I0520100

THE DISAPPEARANCE

BY
J. WAYNE FRYE

An Aaron Adams – Chablis Louise Chavez
Mystery

THE DISAPPEARANCE

THE AUTHOR

Wayne Frye's *Aaron Adams, Girl* series books and *Lynton* adventures are popular among mystery readers. He provides satirical political commentary to many Canadian newspapers, and his books on politics have created a great deal of controversy. He has written marketing/advertising textbooks, been a highly successful U.S. university hockey coach, professor, university president and served as a marketing consultant to hockey teams and motion picture companies. He has been cited for his work with inner-city gang children in the Los Angeles area and been active in the anti-globalization movement. He became a Canadian citizen in 2003 and lives in Ladysmith, British Columbia and Cavite, Philippines.

Other Books by J. Wayne Frye

Hockey Mania and the Mystery of Nancy Running Elk
Something Evil in the Darkness at Hopkins House
How Hockey Saved a Jew From the Holocaust:
The Rudi Ball Story
The Catastrophic Calamities of a Village Idiot
Fighting for Justice in the Land of Hypocrisy
The Girl Who Stirred up the Whirlwind
The Girl Who Motivated Murder Most Foul
The Girl Who Said Goodbye for the Last Time
Fall From Apocalypse
Armageddon Now
Worth
When Jesus Came to Jersey as the Son of Thunder
When Jesus Came to Canada to Lead an Indigenous Rebellion
Canadian Angels of Mercy – Nurses in Times of Peril
Points of Rebellion: Aboriginals Who Fought for Justice
Lynton Walks on Water
Lynton Curls Her Hair
Lynton and the Vampire at Taygaytay Manor
Lynton Buys a Cell-Phone and Hears the Voice of Doom
Chablis: Avenging Angel for the Forgotten
In the City of Lost Hope
Chablis and the Terrorist
Who Resurrected the Spirit of Che Guevara
Pursuit

J. Wayne Frye   2

THE DISAPPEARANCE

TABLE OF CONTENTS

**TO: Brent – Our youth is long gone,
but the memories linger for a lifetime.**

Copyright 2015 by J. Wayne Frye

All rights reserved. No part of this book or covers
may be reproduced or transmitted in any form or by
any other means, electronic or mechanical,
including photocopying, recording, or by any
information storage and retrieval system, without
permission from the author.

This is a work of fiction. Any similarity to persons
living or dead is coincidental.

Catalogue Number: 2014-2453571

ISBN: 978-1-928183-17-4

Fireside Books – Victoria, British Columbia
Part of the Peninsula Publishing Consortium

THE DISAPPEARANCE

PROLOGUE

ENTHRAL AND MYSTIFY

Aaron Adams turned to his friend Brent and said, "You mention a case that I thought had long ago been forgotten. I have not thought about it myself for years, as too many things have been going on in my life the past decade. It has not been a good journey for me recently. We have not seen one another in such a long time and much has happened in my life, unfortunately, probably more bad than good. Ah, but that case is like a fine wine that must be put into the dark recesses of a cellar to mellow and ferment until it is refined with a depth of taste that will titillate the palate and make the taste buds tingle with the ambrosia that sears the soul."

Brent leaned forward slightly, crossed his right leg over his left and with great interest said, "I have been wanting to hear about this case ever since it made headlines in the *New York Times*. I only know what I have read. Pray tell me about it. Share its most intimate details, as you know that I am fascinated and enthralled by a mystery. I lead the boring life of a small town entrepreneur, so titillate my atrophied brain cells a bit."

Now Aaron was universally acknowledged by almost everyone in the know as an astute and skilful man for handling mysterious and unprecedented cases, except for maybe a few who thought his partner, Chablis Louis Chavez, was perhaps a bit younger and more savvy in the modern ways of detecting. Drawing up to the fireplace in the deserted lodge, the two were sitting in lazy enjoyment of one another's company for the first time in decades. Aaron eased back with the satisfied air of a man who had a good story to tell and he prepared to weave it in his usual slow methodical way. This was a tale that took time, and it was one that would enthral and mystify.

THE DISAPPEARANCE

CHAPTER 1

SOMETHING SINISTER
AND FORBODING

Aaron began his tale almost matter-of-factly. "I was one lazy Sunday morning loitering peacefully at my office poring over old files in an attempt to get caught up on work, when the door opened and a reasonably attractive middle-aged woman came in whose agitated air at once attracted my attention. Going up to greet her, I asked what I might do for her."

"A detective," she replied, glancing cautiously about the entire room as if she expected it to be filled with miscreants who might do her mortal harm, "I don't wish anything said about it, but a girl disappeared from our house last night," and she stopped at that point as she was out of breath, her emotion seemingly overcoming her "and I want some one to look for her, but it must be done so very discreetly."

"My dear woman, discretion is guaranteed all our clients. A girl? What kind of a girl; and what house do you mean when you say our house?"

She looked at me keenly before replying. "You are here alone, right?"

"I am alone," I replied.

I shrugged my shoulders and looked up as Chablis (*pronounced Shablee*) walked by the door, causing the woman to panic, as she hunched down, hiding her face. I reassured her and motioned for Chablis to come in.

Confidently, I tried to ease her fears. "It is alright. This is my partner Chablis Louise Chavez. She is the soul of discretion and a more skilled detective does not exist," then I got a slight grin on my lips, as I continued, "except for me, of course."

However, the lady was in no mood for levity. Very seriously, she said "OK, I suppose two detectives are better than one."

Drawing Chablis aside, she whispered a few low eager words which I could not hear.

THE DISAPPEARANCE

Chablis listened nonchalantly for a moment but suddenly made a move which I knew indicated strong and surprised interest. I was about to walk off as I felt the lady might feel more comfortable with Chablis, convinced that someone of her own sex might be better to deal with. Of course, you and I know Chablis is transgendered, but she did not. Just as I was about to turn and leave, Chablis said, "He is the man you want to assess things. He is far better than I am, believe me. Let him go to your house and assess the situation."

"OK, OK, but I want you, too."

I approached the woman. "Where do you come from ma'am," I said very distinctly, as I pointed to a chair for her to have a seat in?

"46 Battie Drive, very near Washington Square."

"And what are the specifics?"

"A girl who cleaned for us disappeared last night in a way to alarm us very much. She was taken from her room." She lowered herself into the chair as she continued, "Yes, snatched, taken from her room. I shall spend whatever it takes to find her. I must find her. I will pay whatever it takes, even if I have to borrow money."

I sat down across from her, and Chablis leaned on my desk as we looked at each other, then her. I said, "Ma'am, you need to go to the police."

Chablis also pointedly said, "Yes, you need the police."

Nervously, she replied, "I, we, well, there are reasons I can't. I prefer not to go into them at this time."

Her manner was so intense, her tone so marked and her words so vehement I, at once, and naturally, asked if the girl was a relative of hers?"

"No," she replied, "not a relative, absolutely not." She then got a pensive look on her face as she continued, "But a dear, very dear friend she is. She was a cleaning girl, but I took her under my wing and she had refinement. She was a lady, if you know what I mean. I tell you it is imperative that she be found."

"OK, we will take the case, but you still should consider going to the police. There are many experienced detectives on the force. I can recommend someone who will take good care of you. He is not in your precinct, but he will make a call and see that you get the best man available. I'll see to it."

THE DISAPPEARANCE

"No, absolutely, positively not - I want you and Ms. Chavez here. Please, I need your help."

"You have it, Miss? Yes, what is your name?"

"I am Clara Luce, personal assistant to Mr. Tom Blake of Blake Industries."

"Ah, the multi-millionaire investor and noted philanthropist. He is known as an eccentric. He lives somewhat modestly right off Washington Square."

"That is he."

I gathered up my top coat from the hall tree in the corner, nodded to Chablis and the three of us left the building, went out into the brisk morning air that had just a tinge of November mist in it and headed toward the subway.

We were in the subway car when she whispered to me, "Nothing must be said about it, nothing at all. I told him so. I told him it was imperative, and he promised secrecy. It can be done without folks knowing anything about it, can't it?"

"We'll do our best. I promise. But I need some facts. What is the girl's name and what makes you think she didn't go out of the house of her own accord?"

"Why everything, she would absolutely not have left without telling me, and then the looks of the room. They all got out of the French doors and went away by the back gate. I saw their footprints in the large groomed area to the left of the balcony stairs – both going and coming."

"Sounds like you are a bit of a detective yourself," I said nonchalantly as Chablis nodded in agreement and I continued, "They, what do you mean they?"

"Why, whoever they were who carried her off."

I must have had a sceptical look on my face, because she continued, "You don't believe me. Believe that she was carried off?"

Chablis interjected, "He means that he needs to survey the scene himself to be sure. That's all."

I then quizzically asked "and what of Mr. Blake? Does he doubt that she was carried off?"

"He didn't seem to doubt it at all."

THE DISAPPEARANCE

I scratched my greying hair. "Did you tell him you thought she had been taken off in this way?"

"Of course, and he agreed that was probably what occurred. In fact, he said that he heard the men talking in her room and just assumed she had some male visitors. We are not prudes Mr. Adams, so having a gentleman over was not reason for concern. Annabelle is a young woman of some beauty, and, of course, she does have admirers I am sure." She got a little mischievous twinkle in her eye as she continued. "However, she, as far as I know, does not entertain two men at a time. So, having two men in her room would be unusual, even one, for that matter."

Chablis is a woman who is extremely sexually liberated, so that part of the story brought a slow smile to her succulent, enticing lips as she asked, "Did she entertain men often?"

"Oh no, not at all, until that night she never had any man in her room. She had no steady boyfriend, so it was not a regular occurrence. Mr. Blake would not tolerate that, I am sure. He is a liberal person, but he does have an expensively furnished home, though not one that is overly ostentatious for someone of his means; consequently, he told her, Annabelle

Anderson, that's her name, to be cautious with whom she brought into the house."

Chablis interjected, "You did not hear the men talking in her room?"

"Yes I did. At first, I thought that it might be the television, but after careful reflecting, no, it was definitely the voices of two men I heard – very muffled they were though, almost whispering."

I asked very calmly, "And when did you hear this?"

"Oh, it must have been after midnight. I have a room down the hall from hers, but I had the door ajar."

"Wait," I said, "tell me where the rooms are, hers and yours."

"Hers is on the second floor at the back of the house, and it has a large balcony with steps to the side that go down into the back yard. My bedroom is the front one, facing toward Washington Square on the same floor, but maybe 25 feet down the hallway. We both have a private bath.

"And what of Mr. Blake? He is not on the same floor as you two?"

THE DISAPPEARANCE

"Mr. Blake has the entire third floor all to himself. It has his bedroom, a very large sitting room, an ornately but tastefully furnished office. There is a private elevator to it in the foyer. It does not stop on the second floor. Just goes straight up."

I looked over at Chablis and we were both thinking the same thing as she asked Clara, "So, there is no door for the elevator on the second floor?"

"No, just a faux wall that covers the shaft – no door, no opening. Mr. Blake designed it that way for privacy."

Again, Chablis and I gave each other a knowing glance. This was information that we would file away in our minds and use at a later date. I then asked, "So, where was Mr. Blake's wife?"

"Oh, he has no wife, sir. There is a long story to that not germane at this time."

"I see," said I.

As we exited the subway at Washington Square and were walking up the steps to the street, Chablis said, "And you were awakened last night by hearing whispering which seemed to come from this girl's room."

"Yes, I at first thought it was the people next door, a townhouse is like that you know. Sound carries through the walls even in expensive ones. I just thought it was the neighbours at first, but kept hearing the whispering and realized it was coming from Annabelle's room. I thought to myself that it was unusual for her to have any men in her room. I mean I am no prude, but it was out of character for her. She is a very good girl, very good."

I knew exactly what Chablis was thinking. She was thinking to herself, "Yeah, good girls like to get kinky on occasion, too."

Again Clara said, "She is a good girl, very good." She was adamant as she continued, "a good a girl I tell you, very good. Don't you dare, either of you, even hint that she is promiscuous. Very good girl, very good girl she is."

"Clara, don't get excited," I said soothingly, "I am not going to impugn her purity, we will take it for granted she is as good as gold, go on. I do not judge people because of their sexuality. That is nobody's business, unless of course, it might have a bearing on this case. Then, I may have to explore it as part of the investigation."

The woman wiped her forehead with a hand that trembled like a leaf. "Where was I?" she said as we walked under the Washington Square arch. "Oh, I heard voices and was surprised and got up and went to her door. The noise I made going down the hall must have startled her, for all was perfectly quiet when I got there. I waited a moment, and then I turned the knob and called her. She did not reply and I called again. Then she came to the door, but did not unlock it."

"What is it? She asked. And I said that I thought I heard talking there and I was frightened. She just said that it must have been next door. I apologized for bothering her and went back to my room. There was no more noise, but the next morning she was nowhere about. Worried, I ask Mr. Blake to use his key to get into her room. She was gone. The balcony French doors were wide open and signs of distress and struggle all around. I knew I had not been mistaken; that there were men with her when I went to her door, and that they had carried her off. As I said, at the bottom of the stairs were some footprints both going and coming. For some reason, they walked through the flower bed."

This time I could not restrain myself. "So, she seemed OK when you went to her room, but then the room shows a sign of a struggle. The door to the balcony is wide open, and there are footprints in the soil at the bottom of the stairs. Still, despite all this she gave no indication she was under duress when you talked to her through the door."

Clara clutched my arm and said, "Don't you believe it," as she continued holding my arm. "I tell you what I say is true, and these burglars or whatever they were carried her off. She is a delicate thing, a lovely delicate thing. I fear for her, fear for her life."

"So, was she a bit more than just pretty," I asked, hurrying the woman along, for more than one passer-by had turned their heads to look at us. The question appeared in some way to give her a shock. She seemed lost in thought.

"Ah, I don't know," she muttered; "some might not think so, I always did; it depended upon the way you looked at her. I looked at her differently I suppose."

For the first time I felt a thrill of anticipation shoot through my veins. Why, I could not say. Her tone was peculiar, and she spoke in a sort of brooding way as though she were weighing something in her own mind; but then her manner had been peculiar throughout. Whatever it was that aroused my suspicion, I determined henceforth to keep a very sharp eye upon Clara and I could tell Chablis was thinking the same way. Levelling a straight glance at her face, I asked her how it was that she came to be the one to inform me of the girl's disappearance. I said, "Doesn't Mr. Blake know anything about you hiring us?"

The faintest shadow of a change came into her manner. "I doubt it," she said, "I mentioned it at breakfast time; but Mr. Blake doesn't take much interest in his servants; he leaves all such matters to me."

"Then he does not know you have come for a detective?"

"No, and if you would be so good as to keep it from him. It is not necessary he should know. I shall let you in the back way. Mr. Blake is a man who never meddles with anything, and values his privacy."

"What did Mr. Blake say this morning when you told him that you thought she might have been kidnapped?"

"Not much of anything. He was sitting at the breakfast table reading his paper. He merely looked up, frowned a little in an absent-minded way, and told me I must manage the servants' affairs without troubling him and that he had done enough and that it was his opinion she just had a wild fornicating party and had decided to take off on a lark with those two men and that she'd be back in a few days pleading not to be fired."

"And you just let it drop? You did not pursue it any further?"

"I must say Mr. Blake does not like publicity, for though by no means a harsh man, he has a reserved, aloof air about him that gives the impression he is above the fray, above the mundane things that the rest of us worry about. He is what some would probably call eccentric."

We were now within sight of the townhouse which was among a row of town homes that spoke of some wealth, but not extravagant wealth. I turned to the Clara, who was now all in a flutter, and asked her how she proposed to get me into the house without the knowledge of Mr. Blake.

"Oh, Mr. Adams, all you have got to do is to follow me through the gate to the kitchen; he won't notice, or if he does will not ask any questions. As I said, he is very private and does not like to be bothered."

Going through the back gate which we got to by a circuitous route behind the homes, we went in through the kitchen door. We were greeted with a smile from the cook who had just taken cinnamon rolls out of the oven and the smell was delightful.

We walked through a corridor into a large foyer where the old fashioned elevator, or as it was probably called a hundred fifty years ago when the home was built, a lift, was just coming down. I expected to see Mr. Blake step out, but it was the maid, who had obviously just taken his lunch up.

The rich rarely dined with the help, so he, no doubt, preferred to sit in his privacy and avoid mingling with the common folk. The rich are that way. Well, most of them anyway. Still, I was impressed that a man of his means lived in only relative luxury not splendorous luxury. In America, the rich were royalty and they flaunted it incessantly in a garish display of superiority. That was something I found strange about a country that liked to act superior when it came to democracy. People don't stop to think that by aggrandizing the rich, they are, in a very subtle way, making those at the top of the economic ladder the royalty in the U.S.A. Why even calling the President Mr. President is an acknowledgement of his exalted status. No democracy should have exalted people.

As we walked up the stairs to the second floor, Chablis and I looked at one another. There was a feeling about the place, or was it about the case. There was something sinister and foreboding at play.

CHAPTER 2

TOO LITTLE TIME
PREACHING LOVE

Clara took us briskly up stairs to the second story back room. As we passed through the halls, I could not but notice how richly appointed but still sombre were the old walnut walls and heavily frescoed ceilings, so different in style and colouring from what one normally sees in the cookie cutter houses that dominate the American landscape that is planned by corporations to maximize profit by minimizing the aesthetics. Many times I had been in the homes of the wealthy as a result of my profession, but I had never crossed the threshold of one like this before, and impervious as I am to any foolish sentimentalities, I felt a certain tinge of despair about the place, though also a degree of awe at the thought of a man with great means living in a 3000 square foot town home, as that was out of the norm for America's wealthy who liked to flaunt their affluence. But once in the room of the missing girl, the affluent nature of the place diminished, as I looked about to see if Ms. Luce was correct or not in her surmises as to the manner of the girl's disappearance. The fact that she had disappeared was likely to prove an affair of some importance. For, let me state the facts in the order in which I noticed them. The first thing that impressed me was, that whatever Clara Luce called her, this was no cleaning girl's room into which I had stepped. Plain as was the furniture, in comparison with the elaborate richness of the walls and ceiling of the hallway, there were still scattered through the room, which was large even for a thirty foot wide house, articles of sufficient elegance to make the supposition that it was the abode of an ordinary cleaning woman open to suspicion. This was the room of a lady who knew elegance and taste. There was no doubt that this woman was well-bred and extremely refined in her tastes. The room literally glowed with a sophisticated elegance.

Clara, seeing my look of surprise, hastened to provide some explanation. "It is the room which has always been used by cleaning women," said she; "but when Annabelle came to us, I thought it would be proper to put her in a nicer room as she seemed so dainty and demure, so I gave her a budget to furnish it to her tastes. She does have good taste doesn't she?"

Chablis offered her observation. "Yes, impeccable taste."

I glanced around at the French Provincial desk in the far corner of the room by the French doors and noticed a vase sitting on it full of partly withered roses, and on the bookshelf by the desk I noticed books by Shakespeare, Poe, Faulkner, Steinbeck and Hemmingway. This girl was no slouch when it came to literature.

"You found the hallway door locked this morning?" I asked, after a moment's scrutiny of the room in which three facts had become manifest: first, that the girl had not occupied the bed the night before; second, that there had been some sort of struggle or surprise, one of the curtains being violently torn as if grasped by an agitated hand, to say nothing of a chair lying upset on the floor with one of its finely hand-turned legs broken; third, that the departure, strange as it may seem, had been by the open French doors.

"Yes," she replied; "but there is a separate entrance as you can see." She pointed at the far wall where there was a door. I walked over, turned the knob and it was locked from the other side. I completely turned and walked to the other door and noticed there was no dead bolt on it.

I said, "So, you just used the master pass key to get in?"

"Yes," she replied, "but there was a chair placed against the door with the back under the knob, but it was easy to push aside."

I stepped over to the French doors and looked out at the meticulously maintained lawn. Chablis said, "It would not be so very difficult for a man to get to and from the street on a dark night, for there is a street light that shines right in the back yard."

Chablis, ever observant, looked about the room, walked over to the closet, stared at the clothes hanging there, turned and said to Clara, "Any of her clothes missing?"

Clara immediately dashed to the closet and rummaged through bureau drawers, after which, she excitedly said, "No, nothing is missing but a wide brimmed hat she liked to wear and a coat." She then paused confusedly as she looked down at the open bureau drawer.

"And what else?" I asked as Chablis moved over beside Clara.

THE DISAPPEARANCE

"Nothing, nothing" she said again as she hurriedly closed the bureau drawer; "only some little meaningless knick-knacks."

"Knick-knacks!" I said. "If she stopped for knick-knacks, she couldn't have gone in any very unwilling frame of mind." And somewhat disgusted with the way things were appearing, I looked over at Chablis who shrugged her shoulders as if we were about to throw up our hands and walk away from the case, but the pleading look on Clara's face deterred me.

"I don't understand it at all" she murmured in an almost whisper, drawing her hand slowly across her forehead. "I don't understand it. But," she went on with strong conviction in her manner, "no matter whether we understand it or not, the case is serious; I tell you so, and she must be found."

I was now even more perplexed, and was beginning to wonder just how much she was not revealing. Still, the mystery was enticing. I said, "Why must? If the girl went of her own accord as most things seem to show, why should you, just her supervisor, take the matter so to heart and insist that there is something nefarious going on here?"

She turned away, uneasily taking up and putting down some little items on the table before her. "Is it not enough that I promise to pay for all expenses which a search will cost, without my being forced to declare just why I should be willing to do so? Am I bound to tell you I love the girl? That I believe she has been taken away by foul means and that to her great suffering and distress? That being fond of her and believing this, I am conscientious enough to put every means I possess at the command of those who will recover her?"

Somewhat shocked at the mention of loving her, the usually more direct of the two of us, Chablis, said, "So, you two were romantically involved?"

Bowing her head a bit, Clara said, "That is none of your business."

Chablis, moved to her, put her hand on her shoulder and said, "There is nothing wrong in loving somebody. There is too little of that in the world. We are not judging you, just trying to get all angles covered in solving this mystery." Chablis then turned to me and said, "That isn't relevant at this point Aaron. Drop it."

Bowing to Chablis instincts, I simply dropped it and brought up another topic. "Mr. Blake, surely he has some interest in finding her. How can he be so callous?"

"I have before said," she retorted, with great conviction, "that Mr. Blake takes very little interest in his servants and affairs of the household. As his administrative assistant, those are my duties. I manage the staff, and that is the way he wants it. He deplores trouble of any kind, absolutely deplores it."

I cast another glance about the room. "How long have you been in this house?"

"I was in the service to Mr. Blake's father for 10 years until he died 7 years ago, and upon his father's death, Mr. Blake said he wanted me to perform the same duties I performed for his father. All together, 17 years."

"And Annabelle. How long has she been here?"

"Oh, it has been almost a year. Yes a year next month."

Although at times considered inappropriate, in an investigation, knowing someone's ethnicity can be important, so I asked, "And what is her ethnic background. I assume she is not white?"

"Oh no, Annabelle is white. Yes, she is dark-skinned but Caucasian. She is far from your common domestic type."

Perplexed, I said, "And what do you mean, Clara, by that? Was she well-educated, had the fine social graces of a more affluent person, etc.?"

"I don't know what to say. She was well-educated, yes, but not as you would call a lady educated. Yet, she knew a great many things the rest of the servants did not know. She liked to read, you can see that," she said as she pointed to the bookshelf. Then she continued, "You can talk to the rest of the staff about her if you like."

I looked intently at the somewhat attractive Clara, a woman of maybe 45 or so, who had the bearing of affluence, but obviously came from working class stock or she would not be a mere domestic lackey for a wealthy eccentric. Was she the mild-mannered person she appeared, or was there something she was hiding?

"Where did you get this girl?" I inquired.

Chablis finished my question "Where did she live before coming here? What is her age? What of her family? What about her references? What of her habits and customs while working here?"

Smiling at Chablis' erstwhile completing of my thoughts, I said. "Yes."

Somewhat bewildered, biting her lip, sighing and taking a deep breath, Clara said, "Frankly, I never asked her any of those questions."

"You hired someone to work in this nice home without checking references. You never got a previous address. Isn't that a bit unprofessional," said Chablis.

"I suppose, yes. You see, she was so nice."

Then I lost my cool. "And pretty."

Chablis immediately barked at me, "Aaron, please!"

I took a deep breath and said, "I'm sorry Ms. Luce. That was an inappropriate response. Please forgive me."

"It's perfectly alright, Mrs. Adams. I completely understand. You are just perplexed by this case and all the limitations I seem to be imposing. You see, I never asked her to talk about herself. She came to me for work and I liked her so much and took her without recommendation. Stupid I know, very stupid. I realize that now, but I was thinking with my heart at the time, not my head."

"And she has served you well all this time?" said Chablis.

"Excellently, the very best she is. I mean incredibly efficient."

"Go out often," I asked.

She shook her head. "Never went out and only had visitors that one night. I think she had no friends in the city."

I was perplexed. "Well," I said, "I must admit this is a complex situation."

I walked over to the French doors, looked out into the backyard and contemplated. As yet there was nothing to show that the girl had come to any harm. So, it maybe was not a serious matter at all. The whole affair was strange and complicated.

It was a dizzy descent down the stairs and they were very narrow. I could see though that once in the yard, it was an easy path to the back gate. It would only take 2 or 3 seconds if you were fleet of foot. Yeah, I thought, a man could do it easily, but a dainty woman might have more difficulty. Baffled at the idea, I turned thoughtfully back, when I beheld something on the side of the left French door about 5 feet up that caused me to pause and ask myself if this was going to turn out to be a tragedy. It was a drop of congealed blood. Further on towards the window was another, and yes, further still, another and another. I even found one upon the very window itself. Bounding into the room, I searched the carpet for further traces. I dropped to my knees as Chablis moved to the French doors and observed what I was doing. She turned, kicked off her heels and started looking closely at the carpet also.

Clara, excitedly said, "What, what is it?"

I pointed to the drops of blood on the window sill. "Do you see that?" I asked.

She uttered an exclamation and just stared at the door. "Blood!" she shouted, and stood there breathing heavily, with rapidly paling cheeks and trembling form. "They have killed her. Oh my, they have killed her."

She was almost in tears. "Do you think it was her blood?" whispered Clara in a horrified tone.

"There is every reason to believe so," I replied, pointing to a spot where I had at last discovered not only one crimson drop but many, scattered over the dark brown carpet beneath me as Chablis offered, "And here are more," when she found them on the carpet also.

"My, it means they have killed her, doesn't it?" said Clara in a whimpering tone. "What are you going to do now?"

"I am going to get to the bottom of this. Find out what happened;" I confidently said as I got up from my knees.

Clara was almost ready to bawl as Chablis walked over and placed her arms around her, patted her gently and kindly on the back and said, "It may only be an injury from a struggle before they left with her. It does not mean she is dead."

"Really, you mean that she may be alive?"

"Of course she may be alive, Clara. Don't jump to conclusions."

Her face lost something of its drawn expression. "Oh, I am so relieved. You mean there is hope?"

Chablis, knowing that the outcome was probably going to be dire, still offered hope. "Of course, don't despair just yet."

Subduing my consternation at this development I employed my time in taking note of such details as had escaped my previous attention. They were not many. The open writing desk on which, however I found no written documents of any kind, only a few sheets of paper near a laptop computer, with a half eaten Zagnut candy bar on the far edge of the desk, almost ready to fall off as though the girl had been interrupted on the computer and eating, perhaps putting the candy bar down hastily without looking where she placed it. There was also a very small trash can by the right side of the desk that was completely empty. In fact, it was spotlessly clean, almost as if it had been emptied of everything and wiped clean with a rag, a cloth, maybe a handkerchief. All in all, relatively few traceable clues were present.

Now, Chablis is young, but a more astute investigator I do not know. She is marvellously equipped as a woman, but as a detective she is a Mona Lisa of intellect. Her presence made me in a pecuniary way much more confident as two heads, especially two relatively competent heads like mine and Chablis', are better than one.

She did not just look around the room, she surveyed it, and I realized as she looked at me what she was going to ask almost immediately. "Clara, what kind of a looking girl was she?" she asked as she gave me a knowing nod. "Do you have a photo?"

Bowing her head almost shamefully, Clara replied, "No photos, no. Stupid I guess, everyone takes photos nowadays with their cell-phones, but I never did, never."

"Then describe her to me, please, Clara, in as much detail as possible," said Chablis as she took out her little pocket spiral notebook from inside her coat and flipped it open, walked over and picked up one of the pens from the desk. As she stood there, she looked down at the Zagnut candy bar and bent over to study it very closely. She held her right hand up in a stopping motion to indicate that Clara should hold off on her description as she studied the candy bar. I just stood still, not wanting to interrupt Chablis when she was in deep thought. She said, "Annabelle was surprised by the intruders. She had the candy bar in her mouth and was taking a bite just as they came in." Then she motioned me over and showed me how the candy bar was uneven on the eaten portion dangling off the table as she said, "Uneven, because she was startled and stopped the biting motion. She may have known the intruders, but she did not expect them I don't believe."

Standing perfectly erect, Chablis then looked with intent of purpose at the now less disturbed Clara and said, "Describe her to me: hair, eyes, complexion, demeanour etc.; you know, in complete detail."

"She was good-looking, but not striking, if you know what I mean. Yet, she had an air of sensuality about her."

"I do," replied Chablis. "Go ahead. What else?"

She had rosy looking cheeks – high cheek bones. As for her eyes, they were blacker than her hair, which was the not deep black but had a real shiny sheen to it. It was, I suppose a light black. She had no loose flesh anywhere; her body was a taunt as an archer's bow." Then you could see a rise in Clara's chest and she began to breathe a bit more heavily as she continued. "Yes, a very alluring body. No disrespect Chablis, but a lot like yours, just a temple of perfection."

Chablis interjected, "Believe me, no offence taken at all Clara. So, she was strikingly alluring, but not what you would call beautiful?"

Again Clara's chest rose up and down, "Very much so, yes. I mean not beautiful but incredibly alluring just as you said."

Chablis, the wheels now rapidly turning in that incredibly furtive mind that was as astutely refined for detecting as any I have ever known, said very deliberately, "We may get a sketch artist and see if we can't get an idea of exactly what she looks like. Alluring is interesting, very interesting, as men find that a cause for interest that titillates their libidos."

I walked toward the French doors and said, "Let's step outside now."

Just then, almost charging through the doorway came a man. I did not have to be introduced. He was dressed to go out and was holding his coat over his right arm that was in front of his stomach. At the sight, we all stood silent, Clara seemingly stunned.

Mr. Blake was an elegant-looking man with an almost military bearing; proud, reserved, and a trifle sombre. As he came towards us, the light shining through the windows at our immediate right, fell full upon his face, revealing a self-absorbed and melancholy expression, I extended my right hand and said, "Mr. Blake, I believe."

He flipped his coat over to his left arm and extended his right hand. "Yes, I am he."

We shook hands as he said, "And who may I ask sir are you and this young lady with you?"

I am Aaron Adams, and this young lady is Chablis Louise Chavez. We are detectives – private. We were notified by Clara that a girl in your employ had disappeared from your house last night in a somewhat strange and unusual way, and we are here to assess the situation. I apologize for the intrusion."

Frowning, he turned to Clara and said, "You think this is necessary?"

She nodded, seeming to find it difficult to speak. He stared at her with an expression of disgust. "I can hardly think such extreme measures are necessary; the girl will doubtless come back, or if not, then replace her. That should be the end of it."

I said, "That is all well and good for you, I suppose, Mr. Blake. However, it is very evident from our preliminary investigation that the girl did not leave alone, and in my opinion, did not leave of her own free will. In fact, the evidence suggests someone may have forced their way in and abducted her."

"OK, OK, I suppose if you think that she was forcibly removed an investigation might be warranted. And I do prefer you handle it rather than the police. I assume you can be discreet?"

Somewhat perturbed by his indifference toward someone perhaps being kidnapped from his home, I gave him a disgusted glare and said, "Perhaps, sir, if you will allow me, I can show you the reasons why we are convinced she was taken against her will."

"I concede that you know what you are doing, Mr. Adams. I am not unacquainted with your exploits. And I have also heard of Ms. Chavez. You are both quiet well-known and respected from what I have read. I am ready to accept your hypothesis she was abducted without troubling me with proof," observed the prim and proper Mr. Blake with a faint show of asperity and almost complete lack of concern for the woman's welfare. "So, if there is anything to see of a startling nature, perhaps I had best yield to your wishes. Whereabouts is this irrefutable evidence you have assessed."

Clara, obviously ill-at-ease that she had apparently upset Mr. Blake with the intrusion of two detectives, displayed a contrite nature through her body language.

He impatiently waved his hand, indicating he would observe the evidence. Suddenly Clara stepped forward and said, "I hardly think you need trouble Mr. Blake to review the evidence. He is a very busy man."

He turned to her and said, "I'll be the judge of that."

She sheepishly bowed her head and as most of those who serve the rich do, she pleadingly and meekly replied, "Yes sir."

Chablis, never one to suffer arrogance passively looked at Mr. Blake and said, "She is only trying to help find out what happened here. She is concerned about Annabelle's welfare. As her employer, I would think you might also be concerned."

He stuck out his chest and said in reply, "I am concerned madam. I just do not get emotional about things," and then he turned toward Clara and continued, "As some people do."

Chablis, who, at this point, was going to work on solving the case with or without a client, because once she had her teeth sunk into something, she was like a pit bull and would not let go, said "OK, that is good to hear, because when I take a case, I see it through to the end, come hell or high water."

Appearing somewhat contrite, Mr. Blake somewhat apologetically, said, "Your tenacity is admirable Ms. Chavez."

Now, though all this, I was just carefully observing the actions and reactions of Mr. Blake, and I couldn't put my finger on it, but I thought he seemed to know more than he was sharing.

Chablis started pointing out the details to Mr. Blake one by one. His top coat was still draped over his left arm as he listened intently at what Chablis was saying.

"An obvious forcible departure from the premises," I said as I moved next to Chablis. "She did not even take time to gather any clothes."

As I said that, Blake moved very deliberately to the bureau and very purposefully pulled out the top drawer where Clara had noticed the knick knacks missing and immediately Clara moved to the bureau and in a very determined and loud voice said, "Just her personal things, sir." Then, she placed her hand on the drawer and quickly closed it as Blake stood there staring at her.

Chablis noticed the two of them staring at one another very intently and said, "Yes, just personal things Mr. Blake and Clara has already observed that she took almost nothing. However, it does appear that some knick knacks are missing. Maybe you should tell us Clara what you mean by knick knacks. I should have asked earlier."

"A locket, a watch that she got for Christmas and Mr. Blake's Christmas gift – a charm bracelet."

Blake looked at Clara disapprovingly and said, "I give all my employees a present for Christmas. Just a friendly gesture for the holidays." Then he looked directly at Clara and continued as if justifying the gift to Annabelle, "Gave you a gift too, didn't I?"

"Oh yes. Yes, and thank you so much," said a grovelling Clara.

Clara stood there in front of the drawer, almost as if she were guarding it. Still, she never took her eyes off Blake, with an almost savage expression seeming to mesmerize him, and uncharacteristically put him in a subservient mode.

Blake took a very long deep breath and averted her eyes by looking over at me and saying, "If that is all you can show me, I think I will proceed to my appointment. Even the blood could just be from a cut she got. I see no reason for alarm. However, the matter does seem to be more serious than I thought, and if you judge it necessary to investigate, as long as the money does not come out of my pocket, why go ahead and investigate. Of course, I hope you will respect my disdain for notoriety of any kind. Please respect that desire. As for the house, it is at your disposal, under the watchful eyes of Ms. Luce, of course. I bid you good day, then."

Chablis and I looked at each other as he left, confirming our general dislike for the rich and arrogant with a knowing glance.

Clara took one long deep breath and stepped away from the bureau. Instantly Chablis walked over and pulled out the drawer she had so visibly protected. A white towel met our eyes, spread neatly out at its full length. Chablis lifted it as I walked over, and we looked beneath. A carefully folded dress of dark blue silk, to all appearance elegantly made, confronted our rather eager eyes. Beside it was a collar of exquisite lace that had a gold breast-pin of a strange and unique pattern attached. A withered bunch of what appeared to have been red roses were meticulously pressed between two pieces of cardboard. We both drew back in some amazement, involuntarily glancing up at Clara.

"I cannot explain." said a very reticent and apologetic Clara, with calmness strangely in contrast to the agitation she had displayed while Mr. Blake had remained in the room. "That those things rich as they are, really belonged to the girl, I have no doubt. She brought them when she came, and they only confirm what I have before intimated: that she was no ordinary cleaning girl, but a woman who had seen better days."

With a low, "Yeah" and another glance at the dark blue dress and delicate collar, Chablis carefully replaced the cloth she had taken from over them, and softly closed the drawer without either of us having laid a finger upon a single article.

Chablis politely excused herself and walked out of the room. I knew exactly where she was going. Blake had left the house, and she was going to take a look in his room – standard procedure in an investigation with a party who was obviously acting a bit suspicious.

Meeting me downstairs as I was interviewing the maid and cook, she smiled, and I saw that whether she was conscious of betraying it or not, she had come upon some clue or at the least fashioned for herself some theory with which she was more or less satisfied.

"A very masculine place, the upstairs, but elegant and refined nonetheless," Chablis whispered in my ear as I stood in the kitchen now. "I think you would find it very interesting."

My curiosity aroused, I excused myself as Chablis started talking to the maid and cook. I stole very stealthily upstairs and was surprised at what I saw. I had prepared myself to behold, a plain, scantily-furnished room opened before me, of a nature between a library and a studio. There was not even a carpet on the polished floor, only a rug, which strange to say was not placed in the centre of the room or even before the fireplace, but on one side, and directly in front of a picture that almost at first blush had attracted my attention as being the only article in the room worth looking at. It was the portrait of a woman, handsome, haughty and alluring; a modern beauty, with eyes of fire burning beneath high piled locks of dark black hair, that were shimmering even in the painting. The gentleman who had been downstairs did not strike me as the type who would be with such a beauty. She was simply captivating.

I was struck with the distance the picture stood out from the wall, and thought to myself that the awkwardness of the framing came near marring the beauty of this otherwise lovely work of art. As for the likeness I was in search of, I found it or thought I did, in the expression of the eyes which were of the same color as Mr. Blake's but more full and passionate; and satisfied that I had exhausted all the picture could tell me, I turned to make what other observations I could, when I was startled by confronting the agitated countenance of Clara Luce who had entered the room so quietly that I did not hear her come in.

"This is Mr. Blake's room," said she with a tone of indignant haughtiness. "No one, absolutely no one ever intrudes on his space, even the servants can only stand in the hallway and leave his meals by the elevator door."

THE DISAPPEARANCE

"I beg your pardon Clara," I said, glancing around in vain for something else that might have caught Chablis' attention. "I was attracted by the beauty of the picture visible through the half open door and stepped in to favour myself with a nearer view and said, "It is very lovely. A sister of Mr. Blake, I assume?"

"No, his cousin," she said as she took my arm and almost forcibly led me out of the room, and she closed the door behind us with a dramatic flair that added a very definite statement that I was not to go in there again.

As we arrived downstairs by the elevator as I asked to ride it, because I said that I was fascinated with old-fashioned lifts, Chablis greeted us in the foyer.

Chablis immediately started a conversation with her that absorbed my complete attention. "So, you want Annabelle found so much you are willing to spend your own money when your rich employer seems basically disinterested in the whole affair and unwilling to expand any effort or spend any money to find her whereabouts. Kind of a strange state of affairs I would say."

She very meekly replied, "As far as I am able yes. I have a few thousand in the bank. I will go with you there right now and give you a suitable retainer. As I said, I will pay whatever it takes, every last dime I have if necessary, but I am not a rich woman, and can only promise you all I have is at your disposal." Her cheeks grew flushed and she seemed a bit agitated as she continued to lavish us with great praise. "I believe that you two are the best. I know your reputations. I know how reliable you are supposed to be. I assure you that it is imperative that Annabelle be found as soon as is humanly possible"

I said with extreme emphasis, "Have you considered that maybe it would be wise to save your money and see if she doesn't come back. Just wait a couple of days and maybe save yourself some money? You can always hire us later."

Somewhat reticent, she replied slowly, deliberately and obviously with a lot of thought, "Well, I know she will come back if she can. I have no doubt about that. This is her home, so no doubt exists."

Chablis, rubbing her forehead as if she was thinking about something, asked, "Did she seem so satisfied here that you are comfortable saying that?"

"She liked it here and liked her job," and then Clara paused, stood completely silent for a few seconds and blurted out, "She loves it here and I love her, so things work out fine."

Chablis looked at me with quizzical eyes, as finally it appeared that Clara was admitting romantic involvement, but Chablis wanted to be sure there was no misunderstanding. So, she looked directly at Clara and said, "Clara. There is nothing wrong with two women having a romantic relationship. But I have to ask you this and I need an honest, straight-forward answer if we are to pursue this case with the full knowledge we need. Were you two romantically involved? A simple yes or no; that is all I need."

Clara took a deep breath, sighed a bit and said, "Yes."

Chablis said, "Now that we have that out of the way. May I ask why the two of you, since you were romantically involved, did not sleep in the same room?"

"I was the one most in love I think, and I knew that Mr. Blake would fire us if he found out."

Then I ask, "Why would she not have screamed, called out, done something to alert you or anyone that she was being taken away against her will?"

At that point, Clara made a bewildering statement. "She was not the kind of woman to make a fuss, so why would she cry out? Maybe she passed out, or there was a gag.

I said, "Possible, but from my experience, I think she was conscious when taken. After all, there are three sets of footprints in the dirt and one that seems pretty small, which would likely be hers. As for the gag, that is possible."

Chablis interjected, "I have to say Clara that you have been less than honest with us so far, and that if we don't have trust in our client, there is little we can do. It is imperative that we know all there is to know, because only then can we truly help you."

Clara bowed her head a bit and said, "I have levelled with you. I didn't to begin with, because I did not know how you would take to us being lovers. After all, this is a nation where same-sex relationships are considered evil by the church, and I just thought maybe you two might have religious convictions that would create conflict."

Chablis laughed and said, "Religious convictions? The only religious convictions we have is that religion spends too much time preaching condemnation and too little time preaching love."

CHAPTER 3

MORE BEWILDERED THAN EVER

Aaron leaned back in his chair and took a deep breath. Brent, now thoroughly enthralled with the tale, asked him to please continue.

"So, as we made it apparent to Clara that we had no concern whatsoever about two people's love lives, she began to open up about the relationship."

Clara said, "You see, we were not avid lovers. It was not an every night thing; although, had it been up to me, it would have been both day and night. I am not ashamed to tell you that I found her more appealing, more exciting and more enticing than any man I have ever been with. You see, she was my first woman, and I never dreamed it possible that I could fall so deeply in love with someone."

Chablis asked if any of the other servants were aware of their love affair.

"No, not that I know of, Chablis. She actually never showed affection. It was one-sided."

"Any idea at all why she would have two men up here at the same time? I mean obviously you were O.K. with her having these callers?"

"Not really. I was appalled as it was uncharacteristic, but truthfully I knew the love was one sided between us. It was just sex to her. I loved her and I suppose I coerced her into the liaison."

After thinking awhile about the one-sided affair, Chablis interjected, "So why would she have not cried out if she was in distress?"

"She was not a girl to make a fuss. If they had killed her outright, she would never have uttered a cry, because she would want to protect me from being harmed."

"Why say they. Are you 100% sure there were two men in the room?"

Without hesitation, Clara said, "I am confident I heard more than one man's voice in her room."

"O.K. Would you know those voices if you heard them again?"

"No."

There was a surprise in this last negative response which made me take notice. I suspected there was something she was still not sharing, so I bore in on her. "Clara, there are other men servants in the house. I have seen them. Would not they have an interest in a pretty young girl?"

Clara's face turned scarlet and she rose from her chair. "I don't believe it," she said. "Harry was a man who knows his place, and I won't hear such things," she suddenly exclaimed; "No, I told him to stay away from her."

I looked at her long and hard. "So, you had told this servant named Harry to stay away from her?"

"Clara," I observed, "it would greatly facilitate matters if you would kindly tell us why you take such an interest in keeping her away from Harry."

"I, I just didn't like the way he was always gawking at her, so I told him very politely that he was not to be around her unless it was absolutely necessary. That's all."

"O.K., we will let it go at that for the time being," I said, "but one glimpse at her background would do more towards setting us on the right track than anything else you could offer. The trouble is I am not sure her real name is Annabelle Anderson. Tell me about how you hired her."

Her face assumed an unmistakable frown. "Have I not told you," said she, "what is known of it? That she came to me about a year ago for work; that I liked her, and so hired her; that she has been with us ever since."

"Then you will not tell us?" exclaimed Chablis.

Her face fell and a look of hesitation crossed it. Her countenance settled again into a resolved expression. "You are mistaken," said Clara. "If Annabelle had a secret, as nearly all girls have, it had nothing to do with her disappearance, nor would knowledge of it help you in any way. I am confident of this."

I decided that she was not a woman to be frightened or cajoled into making revelations she did not think necessary, but I continued my questioning in a different vein. "However, you will at least tell me this: what were the knick knacks she took away with her from her bureau drawer? It was more than you revealed."

"That is not relevant either. I assure you. They were articles of positive value to her, though I assure you of little importance to any one else. All that is shown by their disappearance is the fact that she had a moment's time allowed her in which to collect what she most wanted."

"Well," I said, "you have not given us much to work with, but I am not the man to recoil from anything difficult. If I can discover the whereabouts of this girl I will certainly do it, but without your cooperation it will be difficult."

She bowed her head and said, "I, I…"

"Yes," said Chablis. "Go on."

"She cared for me. I know it."

"O.K, so if she is alive and able to communicate, she will get in touch with you," said Chablis.

I asked, "Does she read any newspapers or magazines?"

Surprised at the seemingly unrelated question, she replied, "Yes, she loves the Village Voice. She reads it without fail every week."

THE DISAPPEARANCE

Chablis knew exactly what I was thinking. She said to Clara, "Then put an ad in the personals under lost connections: Annabelle, please contact Clara immediately. Or you can change it whatever way you like if you want to make it more personal. You might word it as to indicate there would be a reward for anyone who might know her whereabouts just in case someone familiar with what might have happened to her reads it."

"O.K., I will do that."

We left the house bewildered but very interested in the case.

"An affair of some mystery," remarked Chablis, as we halted at the corner to take a final look at the house and its environs. "As it is, what I wouldn't give for her photograph? Black hair, black eyes, white face and thin figure! What a description whereby to find a girl in this great city of New York."

Then, we saw Mr. Blake returning, obviously assuming that his appointment must have been a short one or a failure. "Let us see if his description will be any more helpful," said Chablis, as we both went hurrying towards the advancing figure of that immaculately attired gentleman, to put a few questions to him without Clara's presence.

THE DISAPPEARANCE

Instantly Mr. Blake stopped, looked at us blankly for a moment, and then replied in a dismissive tone, "I have told you all I know."

Chablis, used to having men fawn over her, was surprised that Mr. Blake showed no interest in her. "Oh, I am sure you think you have sir, but we are concerned about exactly how Annabelle appeared. I mean there are no photographs and the description given us by Clara is pretty vague."

"I am sorry if her description isn't to your liking but I have not the remotest idea how the girl looked as I rarely even looked at her. I leave all domestic concerns entirely with Ms. Luce."

Chablis again bowed low and ventured clarification of the question, but almost dismissing her presence, the answer came distinctly to my ears. "Oh, I may have seen her from time-to-time, I can not say about that; I very often run across the servants in the hall; but whether she is tall or short, light or dark, pretty or ugly, I know no more than you do, sir. Then with a dignified nod he inquired, "Is that all?"

Chablis was getting perturbed. "No, that is not all, the girl worked for you all that time, and you don't even notice her? Bullshit!"

Taken aback by Chablis directness, he replied: "I don't concern myself with mundane matters."

Chablis was a woman who could be very directly sarcastic. "Listen asshole, I don't give a fuck about your definition of the mundane. In my book, a possible murder is not mundane. So, you don't remember what a girl who shared your home looks like?"

I decided to slow down Chablis' assault with words. "So, maybe Harry could help. Clara tried to find him but he was not in the house. Any idea where he might be?"

"Harry was an excellent valet, but a trifle domineering, something which I never allow in any one who works for me. I dismissed him this morning and that was the end of it. I know nothing of what has become of him. So, you want to talk to him, good luck. I paid him off in cash and showed him the door."

With that, he simply walked away leaving us there with our jaws dropped in disbelief. I said, "I should not like to get on that man's bad side."

Chablis, really pissed now, said, "Bad side hell. That is the only fucking side that asshole has."

THE DISAPPEARANCE

"If the girl does not turn up of her own accord, or if we do not succeed in getting some trace of her movements, I'll turn you lose on Blake."

Thinking of her famous Filipino friend, demon-fighter Lynton Viñas, and her high heels of death, Chablis said, "If he keeps fucking with me, I'll borrow Lynton's high heels from hell, and ram them so far up his ass I'll tickle his tonsils."

"So, arrogant assholes aside. What is your honest take on this case, Chablis."

"I have come across nothing that was not in plain sight of anybody that had eyes to see it," she replied.

I shook my head slightly mortified, because she always had the ability to see things others didn't. "You had it all before you and you were not able to pick up anything extraordinary? That in itself is extraordinary."

More nettled than I would be willing to confess, I walked back with her to the subway station, saying nothing. Bidding her goodbye, I hunted up the policeman who had patrolled the district the night before. I inquired if he had seen any one go in or out of the side gate of Mr. Blake's house.

"No," he said, "but I heard Officer Thompson tell a curious story this morning about some one he had seen."

"What was it?"

"He said he was passing that way last night about twelve o'clock when he remarked standing under the lamp near the square, a group consisting of two men and a woman, who no sooner beheld him than they separated, the men drawing back into the dark and the woman coming hastily towards him. Not understanding the move, he stood waiting her approach, when instead of advancing to where he was, she paused at the gate of Mr. Blake's house and lifted her hand as if to open it, when with a wild and terrified gesture she started back, covering her face with her hands, and before he knew it, had actually fled in the direction from which she had come. A little startled, he advanced and looked through the gate before him to see if possible what had alarmed her, when to his great surprise, he beheld the pale face of the master of the house, Mr. Blake himself, looking through the bars from the other side of the gate. He in his turn started back and before he could recover himself, Mr. Blake had disappeared. He says he tried the gate after that, but found it locked."

"Name of who told you this."

THE DISAPPEARANCE

"Officer Thompson."

"Well," I said, "it is interesting, but that is all. Thanks."

However, I did get a description of the girl as relayed to him by Thompson. He said, "The girl appeared to be tall and thin, and was closely wrapped about in a shawl. Long light dark hair and walked with a confident stride."

I thanked him and left the precinct as he headed off to his four o'clock shift. My next move was to make such inquiries as I could with safety into the private concerns of Mr. Blake and his family, and discovered such facts as these:

That Mr. Blake was a man who if he paid but little attention to domestic affairs was yet rarely seen out of his own house, except upon occasions of great political importance, when he, as a Republican Councilman, was always to be found on the platform at meetings of his constituents. Though to the ordinary observer a man eminently calculated, from his good looks, fine position, and solid wealth to enjoy society, he not only manifested a distaste for it, but even went so far as to refuse to participate in the social dinners of his most intimate friends; the only table to which he would sit down being that of some private restaurant, where he was sure of finding none but his political associates assembled.

To all appearance he wished to avoid the ladies, a theory borne out by the fact that never, even in church, on the street, or at any place of amusement, was he observed with one at his side. This fact in a man, relatively young, as he was around 40, rich, and marriageable, would, however, have been more noteworthy than it was if he had not been known to be eccentric. His father had been a known bibliomaniac but was well-known for treating people with contempt. It was whispered in my ear by one gentleman, a former political colleague of Mr. Blake's, that he was known at one time to show considerable attention to his cousin Miss Evelyn Blake, that cousin of his in the portrait, who married a much older man and straightway lost him by death, leaving her fabulously wealthy.

Remembering the picture I had seen in Mr. Blake's private apartment, I asked the source if this lady was a brunette, and being told she was, and of the most pronounced type, felt for the moment I had stumbled upon something in the shape of a clue; but upon resorting to Chablis with my information, she shook her head with a short laugh and told me I would have to dive deeper than that if I wanted to fish up the truth lying at the bottom of the well.

THE DISAPPEARANCE

Meanwhile all our efforts to obtain information in regard to the fate or whereabouts of the missing girl had so far proved utterly futile. Even the advertisements inserted by Clara had produced no effect; and frustrated in my scheme I began to despair, when the accounts of Clara's strange and unaccountable behaviour during the days of suspense, which came to me through Fanny, the pretty housemaid at Mr. Blake's, whose acquaintance I had lately taken to cultivating, aroused once more my dormant energies and led me to ask myself if the affair was quite as hopeless as it seemed.

Fanny said of Clara in an exactingly precise manner, "she couldn't go about this house more than she does. It seems as if she can't keep still a minute, upstairs and down, upstairs and down. And she is always trembling! Her hands are constantly shaking. She also hangs about Mr. Blake's door when he is at home. She never goes in, that was the oddest part of it, but strangely walks up and down before it, wringing her hands and talking to herself just like a mad woman."

In face of facts like those I felt it would be pure insanity to despair. Let there be but a mystery, though it involved a man of the position of Mr. Blake and I was safe. My only apprehension had been that the whole affair would dissolve itself into an ordinary elopement or some such common-place matter.

I discovered that Blake was going to a charity ball. I determined to follow him and learn if possible what change had taken place in himself or his circumstances to lead him into such an innovation upon his usual habits. Though the hour was late I had but little difficulty in carrying out my plan.

The crowd was great and I circulated the floor three times before I came upon him. When I did, I own I was slightly disappointed; for instead of finding him as I anticipated, the centre of an admiring circle of ladies and gentlemen, I spied him withdrawn into a corner with a bland old politician, discussing, as I presently overheard, the merits and demerits of a certain Smith who at that time was making some disturbance in the party.

If that is all he had come for, I thought I would have been better off staying at his home and trying my hand at getting Fanny's pants off. And somewhat chagrined, I took up my stand near by, and began scrutinizing the ladies.

Suddenly I felt my heart stand still, the noise of voices ceasing the same instant behind me. A lady was passing on the arm of a foreign-looking gentleman, whom it did not require a second glance to identify with the subject of the portrait in Mr. Blake's house. Even more magnificent looking than when her picture was painted, her beauty had assumed a certain defiant expression that sufficiently betrayed the fact that the years had not been so wholly happy. There was a look of latent scorn that burned in her dark eyes, as she slowly turned her richly bejewelled self towards the corner where Blake stood, and meeting his eyes no doubt, bowed with a sudden loss of self-possession that seemed to interrupt the haughty carriage of her noble form, held doubly erect for the next few moments, and you could see she was quietly concealing something within.

"She loves him," I inwardly commented and turned to see if the surprise had awakened any expression on Blake's uncommunicative countenance.

Evidently not, for the tough politician of the Fifteenth Ward to whom Blake was conversing, was laughing, at one of his own jokes probably, and looking up in the face of Mr. Blake, whose back was turned to me, in a way that entirely precluded all thought of any tragic expression in that quarter. Somewhat disgusted, I withdrew and followed the lady.

I could not get very near. By this time the presence of a live countess in the assembly had become known, and I found her surrounded by a swarm of half-fledged youths who were buzzing like bees for her attention even though she was escorted. But I cared little for this; all I wanted to know was whether Mr. Blake would approach her or not during the evening.

Tediously the moments passed; but a detective on duty, or on fancied duty, succumbs to no weariness. I had a woman before me worth studying and the time could not be thrown away. I learned to know her beauty; the poise of her head, the flush of her cheek, the curl of her lip, the glance—yes, the glance of her dark, mysterious eyes, though that was more difficult to understand, for she had a way of drooping her lids at times that, while exceedingly effective upon the poor wretch toward whom she might be directing that half-veiled shaft of light, was anything but conducive to my purposes.

At length, with a restless shrug of her haughty shoulders, she turned away from her crowd of adorers, her huge breasts rising up and down provocatively under a tight fitting garment, and her whole face flaring with a light that might mean resolve and might mean simply contempt. I had no need to turn my head to see who was advancing towards her; her stately attitude of interest, her thrilling glance as woman, betrayed that only too readily.

THE DISAPPEARANCE

Blake was the more composed of the two. Bowing over her hand with a few words I could not hear, he drew back a step and began uttering the usual common-place sentiments of the occasion.

She did not respond. With a splendour of indifference not often seen even in the manner of the grandest ladies, she waited, but for what? Finally she said, "I know all this has to be gone through with, therefore I will be patient."

But as the moments passed, and his tone remained unchanged, I could detect a slight gleam of impatience flash in the depths of her dark eyes, and a change come into the conventional smile that had hitherto lighted, without illuminating her countenance. Drawing still further back from the crowd that was not to be awed from pressing upon her, she looked around as if seeking a refuge. Her glance fell upon a certain window, with a gleam of satisfaction. Seeing they would straightway withdraw there, and wanting to make certain that Blake did not recognize me, I took advantage of the moment and made haste to conceal myself behind a large pillar as near that vicinity as possible. In another instant I heard them approaching.

"You seem to be rather overwhelmed with attention tonight," were the first words I caught, uttered in Mr. Blake's calmest and most courteous tones.

"Do you think so?" was the slightly sarcastic reply. "I was just deciding to the contrary when you came up."

There was a pause. He was eyeing her intently; a firm look upon his face that made its reserve more marked than common. I saw him gaze at her handsome head piled with its midnight tresses amid which the jewels, doubtlessly provided by her dead husband, burned with a fierce and ominous glare, at her smooth olive brow, her dark eyes where the fire passionately blazed, at her scarlet lips trembling with an emotion her rapidly flushing cheeks would not allow her to conceal. I saw his glances fall and embrace her whole elegant form with its casing of ruby velvet and ornamentation of lace and diamonds, and an expectant thrill passed through me almost as if I already beheld the mask of his reserve falling, and the true man flash out in response to the wooing beauty of this full-blown rose, evidently in waiting for him. But it died away and a deeper feeling seized me as I saw his glances return enkindled to her countenance, and heard him say in still more measured accents than before: "Is it possible then that you could desire the adulation of one who is your distant cousin?"

THE DISAPPEARANCE

Slowly her dark eyes turned towards him; she stood like a statue.

"But I forget," he went on, a tinge of bitterness for a moment showing itself in his smile, "perhaps in returning to Manhattan, Evelyn Blake has so far forgotten the last years as to find pleasure again in place where she spent her youth." And he bowed almost to the ground in his half sarcastic homage.

"Evelyn Blake! It is long since I have heard that name," she murmured.

He could not restrain the quick flush from mounting to his brow. "Pardon me, if it brings you sadness or unwelcome memories."

A smile crossed her lips grown suddenly pallid. "You are mistaken," she said. "If my name brings up a past laden with bitter memories and shadowed by regret, it also recalls much that is pleasant and never to be forgotten. I do not object to hearing my maiden name uttered by one of my relatives."

The answer was dignity itself. "Your name is Mrs. Devore, your relatives must be proud to utter it."

A gleam not unlike lightning's quick flash shot from the eyes, "Is it Tom Blake I am listening to," she said, "I do not recognize my old friend in the cool and sarcastic man of the world now before me."

"We often fail to recognize the work of our own hands, after it has fallen from our grasp."

"What," she cried, "do you mean?"

"I would say nothing," he replied calmly. "At a meeting which is at once a meeting and a parting, I would give utterance to nothing which would seem like recrimination."

"Wait," suddenly she exclaimed, "you have spoken a word which demands explanation; what have I ever done to you that you should speak the word recrimination to me?"

"What? You shook my faith in womankind; you showed me that a woman, who had once told a man she loved him, could so far forget that love as to marry one she could never respect, for the sake of money."

"What," she said, this time without gesture or any movement, save that of her lips grown pallid as marble, "and what did you show me?"

He started, profoundly, and for a moment stood before her unmasked of his stern self-possession. "I beg your pardon. I am sorry."

THE DISAPPEARANCE

She lifted her head and surveyed him. With glance less cool than his, but fully as deliberate, she looked at his proud head bending before her; studying his face, line by line, from the stern brow to the closely compressed lips on which melancholy seemed to have set its everlasting seal, and a change passed over her countenance. "Tom," she said, with a sudden rush of tenderness, "if in the times gone by, we both behaved with too much worldly prudence for it now to be any great pleasure for either of us to look back, is that any reason why we should mar our whole future by dwelling too long upon what we are surely still young enough to bury if not forget? I acknowledge that I would have behaved in a more ideal fashion, if, after I had been forsaken by you, I had not sought solace in riches. But I was young, and riches had its charms, so did the prospect of wealth and position, which I was now not going to get by marrying you, make me anything but a predator? Yes, I was a predator, but I was in so much pain when you said even fourth cousins should not marry."

"Impossible," he replied, his whole face darkening. "What was done at that time cannot be undone. For you and me there is no future. Yes," he said turning towards her as she made a slight fluttering move of dissent, "no future; we can bury the past, but we can not resurrect it. I doubt if you would wish to if we could; as we cannot, of course, you will not desire even to converse upon the subject again. Evelyn, I wanted to see you once, but I do not wish to see you again; will you pardon my plain speaking, and release me from this agony I feel."

"I will pardon your plain speaking my dear Tom, but..." Her look said she would not release him.

He seemed to understand it, and smiled, but very bitterly. In another moment he had bowed and gone, and she had returned to her crowd of adoring admirers, and I was more confused than ever. I kept asking what baring this might have on the case. I did not know, but it was damn interesting.

Chablis and I were barrelling through poor Clara's money rapidly, so I decided to foot the bill for some of the expenses myself. I explained to Clara that there was something dark and sinister about Blake, and that I had just an inkling that he knew more than he was divulging. She seemed taken aback, and insisted there could not be any connection between Blake and the disappearance. I asked her politely if she was sure she wanted to pursue this further, as I was a man who always let the chips fall where they may. She sighed and seemed to actually be giving it some deep thought, but shook her head and replied, "No, do what you must. I need to know what happened to Annabelle."

I needed to be close to the house for I sensed very deeply that something dark and sinister was going on in that place, so I rented a room in a boarding house down the lane from the Blake home. My room, as I took pains to have it, overlooked the avenue, and from its windows I could easily watch the goings and comings of the gentleman whose movements were daily becoming of more and more interest to me. His restlessness at this period was truly remarkable. Not a day did he not spend his time in walking the streets, and that not in his usual aimless gentlemanly fashion, but eagerly and with an intent gaze that roamed here and there, like a bird seeking its prey. It would often be as late as five o'clock before he came in, and if, as frequently happened, he did not have company to dinner, he would start out again after seven o'clock and go over the same ground as in the morning, looking with strained gaze, that vainly endeavoured to appear unconcerned, into the faces of the women that he passed. I not infrequently followed him at these times as much for my own amusement as from any hope I had of coming upon anything that should aid in the work before me. But when he suddenly changed his route of travel from a promenade in the fashionable thoroughfares of Broadway and Fourteenth Street to a walk through

THE DISAPPEARANCE

Chatham Square and the dark, winding, narrow streets of the East side, I began to observantly scent whom the prey might be that he was seeking, and putting every other consideration aside, regularly set myself to dog his steps, as only I, with my innumerable disguises and ability to fawn various mannerisms, knew how to do.

For three separate days I kept at his heels wherever he went, each day growing more and more astonished if not to say hopeful, as I found myself treading the narrowest and most disreputable streets of the city; halting at the shops of pawnbrokers; peering into the back-rooms of dive-type bars; mixing with the crowds that infest the teaming streets of despair at nightfall, and even slinking with hand on the trigger of the pistol I carried in my pocket, up dark alleys where every door that swung noiselessly to and fro as we passed, shut upon haunts of villainy hatched in a world where survival depended on staying one step ahead of the police. At first I thought Mr. Blake might have some such reason for the peculiar course he took. But his indifference to all crowds where men predominated, his silence where a word would have been well received, convinced me it was a woman he was seeking and that with an intentness that bordered on the fanatical. I even saw him once in his hurry and abstraction, step across the body of a child who had fallen face downward on the concrete and that with an expression showing he was utterly unconscious of anything but an obstacle in his path. Then again, this was not that unusual I suppose in a nation that cared so little for those in poverty.

The strangest part of it all was that for a man of wealth he seemed to have no fear, mingling with those who had been stomped into oblivion by the cruellest economic system ever perpetrated on mankind. To be sure he took pains to leave his valuables at home obviously, but to the poor and dispossessed, the eye can always adequately assess a man of wealth, and those he went among would do anything for money. Still he never displayed any fear. Perhaps, like me, he carried a pistol. At all events he shunned no spot where either poverty lay hid or deviltry reigned, his proud stern head bending to enter the lowest doors without a tremble of the haughty lips that remained compressed as by an iron force; except when some poor forlorn creature with tremulous hands, attracted by his bearing, would hastily brush against him, when he would turn and look, perhaps speak, though what he said I always failed to catch; after which he would hurry on as if possessed by demons. The evenings of those three days were notable also. Two of them he spent in the manner I have described; the third he went to the Windsor

THE DISAPPEARANCE

House Hotel in Soho, where Evelyn Blake was staying, going up and down in the lobby, only to start back with his hands behind his back, and his head bent, evidently deliberating as to whether he should or should not have the clerk ring her room. The arrival of a taxi when he went outside changed his demeanour. The door to the cab opened, and I saw him cast one look at her and shrink back with what appeared to be a sigh of anger or disgust, and without waiting to greet her, he turned toward home with a vigorous step that made it difficult for me to keep up with him.

The fourth day to my infinite chagrin, I was summoned by Chablis to appear in court on another case we were working on. When I returned, Blake was gone, but I eye Clara who seemed to be unusually restless, opening the windows and looking out with a forlorn look. Indeed I have no doubt from what I afterwards learned, that she was in a state of constant suspense during those days. Her frequent calls to Chablis, where she in vain sought some news of the girl in whose fate she was so absorbed, confirmed this. Only the day before I gave myself up to my unreserved espionage of Mr. Blake, she had visited Chablis and let fall her apprehensions that the girl was dead, and asked whether if that were the case, the police should be contacted. Upon being assured that if she had not been privately made away with, there was every chance we would find her as we were working on leads, made her grow a little calmer, but before going away had so far forgotten herself as to intimate that if some result was not reached soon she should take the matter into her own hands, whatever that meant.

It was no wonder, then, that her countenance bore marks of the keenest anxiety as she trod the halls of that dim semi-mansion, with its dusky corners rich with bronzes and the glimmering shine of ancient brocades, breathing suggestions of loss and wrong; or bent her wrinkled forehead to gaze from the windows for the coming of one whose footsteps were ever delayed. She happened to be looking out, when after a longer stroll than usual the master of the house returned. As he made his appearance at the corner, I saw her hurriedly withdraw her head and hide herself behind the curtain, from which position she watched him as he passed up the steps and entered the house. Not until the door closed after him, did she venture to issue forth and with a hurried movement shut the blinds and disappear.

To ferret out this mystery, I still found myself forced to admit the possibility of there being none at all. It had now become the one ambition of my life; and all because it was not only an unusually blind one, but of a nature that involved me with a zest rare even to me who loves my work and all it involves with an undivided passion.

To equip myself, then, in a fresh disguise and to join Mr. Blake shortly after he had left his own corner, was anything but a hardship to me that next morning, though I knew from past experience, a long and wearisome walk was before me with nothing in all probability at the end but reiterated disappointment. But for once the fates had willed it otherwise. Whether Mr. Blake, discouraged at the failure of his own attempts, whatever they were, felt less heart to prosecute them than usual I cannot say, but we had scarcely entered upon the lower end of the Bowery, before he suddenly turned with a look of disgust, and gazing hurriedly about him, hailed a Madison Avenue cab that was rapidly approaching but just as he was about to get in, he stepped hastily back and with his eyes upon a girl who was hurrying past him with a package in her arms. I saw him draw aside the girl, who from her garments was afflicted with that malady that grows like a disease in capitalism, poverty. After talking earnestly with her for a few moments, he walked by her side down the street, still talking. I hasted after them, when I was suddenly disconcerted by observing him hurriedly separate from the girl and turn towards me. Weighing in an instant the probable good to be obtained by following either party, I determined to leave Mr. Blake for one day to himself, and turn my attention to the girl he had addressed, especially as she was tall and thin and bore herself with an extremely confident stride not generally given to the poor who seem to slump in shame at an affliction they cannot help.

Barely bestowing a glance upon him, then, as he passed, in a vain attempt to read the sombre expression of his inscrutable face grown five years older in the last five days, I shuffled after the girl now flitting before me down the street. As I did so, I noticed her dress in minute detail, somewhat surprised to find how ragged and uncouth it was. That Mr. Blake should stop a girl like this was a riddle to me. I hastened forward with intent to catch a glimpse of her countenance if possible; but she seemed to have acquired wings to her feet since her rendezvous with Blake. Darting into a crowd, she sped from my sight with such rapidity, I soon saw that my only hope of overtaking her lay in running. I accordingly quickened my steps but lost her in a crowd.

When I came back to my room that afternoon, I was exhausted and fell asleep on the sofa. The next morning Blake did not start out as usual, and at noon I received intimation from Fanny, one of the maids, that he was preparing to take a journey. Where, she could not inform me, nor when, though she thought it probable he would take an early train. Clara was feeling dreadfully, she informed me; and the house was like a grave. Greatly excited at this unexpected move on Blake's part, I went home and packed a suitcase.

The truth was, I had travelled so far and learned so little, that my professional pride was wounded. Blake stepped up to the ticket office at Grand Central Station the next morning to buy a ticket for Bellow Falls, a small town in the southern part of Vermont. He found beside him a young man of maybe 20, who by some strange coincidence wanted a ticket for the same place. The fact did not seem in the least to surprise him, nor did he cast me a look beyond the ordinary glance of one stranger at another. I was wearing my moustache and raised forehead disguise but wondered if he recognized me, despite the quick glance. Blake had no appearance of being a suspicious man, nor do I think at this time, he had the remotest idea that he was either watched or followed; an ignorance of the truth which I took care to preserve by taking my seat in a different car and not showing myself again during the whole ride to Vermont. Each passing day made me realize that there was something deeply sinister going on in the Blake household. I called Chablis and said, "In Vermont and am more bewildered than ever."

CHAPTER 4

DID FOR THE NEXT 15 MINUTES

Why Blake should take a journey at all at this time, and why of all places in the world he should choose such an insignificant town as Bellow Falls for his destination, was of course the mystery upon which I brooded during the entire distance. But when somewhere near five in the afternoon, I stepped from the cars on to the platform at the station only to hear Tom Blake making inquiries in regards to how to get to the small village nearby of Saxton's Bend further east. As he was told there was a passenger van went there only in the mornings and returned at 9:00PM, he seemed severely disappointed.

.

"You will have to wait till tomorrow I fear," said the ticket agent, "unless you can find someone going that way and hitch a ride."

THE DISAPPEARANCE

When he asked directions to the only hotel in town, I did not wait to hear more but hurried down to the hotel. I took a seat in an old dilapidated dusty chair and waited behind a newspaper I picked up that was over a week old.

The prospect of a tedious evening spent in a country hotel was most unendurable to me, but after he checked in and went to his room, I did the same. After getting settled I made some inquiries and found Blake was completely unknown in the town as far as I could surmise.

I had secured the next room to his, and I spent a sleepless night listening to Blake pace the floor. I had already arranged a car through the hotel desk clerk for the next day and it was delivered that night as the man said it didn't matter as no one every rented a car anyway as he just did it as a convenience for people who had him do repair work on their cars at his service station. It was a candidate for Rent-A-Wreck back in the days when they were first in business as it was actually an old 1971 Datsun with stick shift that lurched violently every time you put it in second gear.

Early the next morning Blake took the van and I pulled in behind it, following relatively close. There were other passengers, but I noticed he never spoke to any of them, nor through all the long drive did he once look up and out the window. It was twelve o'clock when we reached the end of the route, a small town of somewhat less than the usual pretensions of mountain villages; so insignificant indeed, that I found it more and more difficult to imagine what the wealthy Blake could find in such a spot as this, to make amends for a journey of such length and discomfort; when to my increasing wonder I saw him after dinner hand a man some money and get in his car.

I tailed him from far behind. We passed a miniscule green sign that said Saxton's Bend Village, and I assumed that was where he was headed.

He got out of the car by an old winding desolate dirt road that seemed to lead nowhere. He looked back my way, but apparently discounted any concern that he was being followed. I parked and waited awhile and walked toward the dirt road very cautiously looking down it and I saw him in the far distance. I ducked into the adjacent woods for cover and continued to follow.

It was not long before I saw him make a swift turn and head back in my direction. I hunkered down in the forest and waited. He walked by me back to the main road, turned right and started walking up it. Obviously, he had simply been trying to divert anyone who might be following him from his real intentions.

And thus we went on for an hour, over the most uneven country I ever traversed, he always one hill ahead; when suddenly, by what instinct I cannot determine, I felt myself approaching the end, and hastening to the top of the ascent up which I was then labouring, looked down into the shallow valley spread out before me.

What a sight met my eyes if I had been intent on anything less practical than the movements of the solitary man below! Hills on hills piled about a verdant basin in whose depths nestled a scanty collection of houses, in number so small they could be told upon the fingers of the right hand, but which notwithstanding lent an indescribable aspect of comfort to this remote region of hill and forest.

Blake pausing half way down the slope before me, examining, yes examining a small pistol, which he held in his hand, soon put a big question mark in my head about what I was witnessing. Somewhat alarmed I reined back; but his action had evidently no connection with me, for he did not once glance behind, but kept his eye on the road which I now observed took a short turn towards a house in the distance.

THE DISAPPEARANCE

Situated on a level track of land at the crossing of three roads, its spacious front, crude and unpainted as it was, presented every appearance of an inn, but from its moss-grown chimneys no smoke arose, nor could I detect any sign of life in its shutter-less windows and closed doors, across which shivered the dark shadow of several pines, that stood like guards beside its tumbled-down porch.

Blake seemed to have been struck by the same fact concerning its loneliness, for hurriedly replacing his pistol in his breast pocket, he moved slowly forward. I instantly conceived the plan of striking across the belt of underbrush that separated me from this old dwelling, and by taking my stand opposite its front, intercept a view of Blake as he approached. Hastily, I rambled into the bushes, proceeding to carry out my plan. I was so far successful as to arrive at the further edge of the wood, which was thick enough to conceal my presence without being too dense to obstruct my vision, just as Blake passed on his way to this solitary dwelling. He was looking very anxious, but determined. Turning my eyes from him, I took another glance at the house, which by this movement I had brought directly before me. It was even more deserted-looking than I had thought; its unpainted front with its double row of blank windows meeting your gaze without a response, while one huge old pine with half its limbs dismantled of foliage, rattled its old bones against its sides and moaned in its aged fashion like a ghost crying in the dark.

Blake walked up to the front door and knocked, without hesitation, on its dismal panels with his left hand. No response was heard. He tried the latch: the door was locked. Hastily running his eye over the face of the building, he walked around the house, which he could easily do owing to the absence of every obstruction in the way of fence or shrubbery. Finding no means of entrance, he returned again to the front door which he shook with an impatient hand that however produced no impression upon the trusty lock, and recognizing, doubtless, the futility of his endeavours, he proceeded with sombreness and clouded brow to leave.

This old inn or decayed homestead was then the object of his lengthened and tedious journey; this ancient house rotting away among the bleak hills of Vermont. I could not understand it. Rapidly emerging from the spot where I had secreted myself, I in my turn made a circuit of the house, if happily I should discover some loophole of entrance which had escaped his attention. However, every door and window was securely barred, and I was about to follow his example and leave the spot, when I saw two or three children advancing towards me down the cross roads, gaily swinging their arms. I noticed they hesitated and huddled together as they approached and saw me, but not heeding this, I greeted them with a pleasant word or so, then pointing over my shoulder to the house behind, asked who lived there. Instantly their already pale faces grew paler.

"Why," cried one, a boy, "don't you know? That is where the two wicked men lived who stole the money out of the Rutland bank. They were put in prison, but they escaped."

Here, the other, a little girl, plucked him by the sleeve with such affright that he, himself, took alarm and just giving me one quick stare out of his wide eyes, grasped his companion by the hand and took to his heels. As for myself I stood rooted to the ground in my astonishment. This dilapidated, sleepy old house had been the home of the notorious Shoemans, who had boldly robbed a bank in Rutland, killed three of the tellers, had a shootout with arriving police and killed two of them while leading them on a wild chase before finally escaping. They were eventually found and sentenced to life in prison where they had escaped killing two guards in the process. That had been about six weeks ago. Bewildered, confused and confounded and I just stood there staring off into space. After awhile, I started walking back toward my car, more perplexed than ever.

THE DISAPPEARANCE

Looking back, I eyed the house once more. How altered it looked to me! What a murderous aspect it wore, and how dismally secret were the tight shut windows and closely fastened doors, on one of which a rude cross scrawled in red chalk met the eye with a mysterious significance. Even the old pines had acquired the villainous air of the uncanny repository of secrets too dreadful to reveal, as they groaned and murmured in the building wind. Dark deeds and foul wrong seemed written all over the fearful place, from the long strings of black moss that clung to the worm-eaten eaves, to the worn stone where the killers had trampled as children. Suddenly with the quickness of lightning the thought flashed across me, what could the aristocratically arrogant Blake, have wanted in that nest of infamy? What errand of hope, fear, despair, avarice or revenge, could have brought him and his refined tastes and proudly reticent manners, so many kilometres from home, to the forsaken den of hardy villains whose name now, had stood as the type of all that was bold, bad and lawless, and for whom during the last few weeks the cry for retribution had been ballyhooed. Contemplation brought no reply, and shocked at my own thoughts I put the question by for steadier brains than mine; and instead of trying further to solve it, cast about how I was to gain entrance into this deserted building as I turned and walked back; for to enter it I was more than ever determined, now that I had heard to whom it had once belonged.

Examining with a glance the several roads that branched off in every direction from where I stood, I found them all equally deserted. Even the children had disappeared in one of the four or five houses that were scattered in the remote distance.

If I was willing to enter upon any daring exploit, there was no one to observe or interrupt. I resolved to make the attempt with which my mind was full. This was to climb the old tree next to the house, and from one of the two or three branches that brushed against the house, gain entrance through a window that stared at me from amid the pine's dark needles. Taking off my coat with a sigh, I bent my energies to the task, a difficult one indeed for a man my age. With little more than a scratch or so, I reached the window of which I have spoken, and after a moment spent in regaining my breath, saw that it was not even latched. I alighted upon a heap of broken glass in a large bare room. An ominous chill at once struck my heart. Though I am anything but a sensitive man as far as physical impressions are concerned, there was something in the hollow echo that arose from the four blank walls about me as my feet alighted on that rough, uncarpeted floor that struck a vague chill through my blood, and I actually hesitated for the moment whether to pursue the investigations I had promised myself, or beat a hasty retreat. A glance at the huge distorted limbs swaying across the square of the open window decided for me. It was easy to enter by means of that unsteady support, but it would be extremely unsafe to venture out in that way. If I prized life and limb I must seek some other method of egress. I, at once, put my apprehensions in my pocket and entered upon my self imposed task.

I surveyed the room meticulously. Two or three old chairs piled in one corner, a rusty stove, a heap of tattered and decaying clothing, were all that met my gaze. Taking my way, then, toward the door, I opened it and saw a stairway. I proceeded to descend into what to my excited imagination looked like a gulf of darkness. It proved, however, to be nothing more nor less than an unlighted hall at the bottom of small dimensions, with a another stair-case at one end and a door at the other, which, upon opening I found myself in a large, square room with an immense four-post bed. There were articles in the room; a disused bureau, a rocking chair, even a table, but nothing had such a ghostly look as that antique bed with its curtains of calico tied back over its naked framework, like rags draped from the bare bones of a skeleton. Passing hurriedly by,

THE DISAPPEARANCE

I tried a closet door or so, finding little, however, to reward my search; and eager to be done with what was every moment becoming more and more disappointing, I hastened across the floor to the front of the house where I found another hall and a row of rooms that, while not entirely stripped of furniture, were yet sufficiently barren to offer little encouragement to my curiosity. One only, a small but not uncomfortable room, showed any signs of having been occupied within a reasonable length of time; and as I paused before its hastily spread bed, thrown together as only a man would do it, and wondering why the room was so dark, looked up and saw that the window was entirely covered by an old shawl and a couple of heavy coats that had been hastily nailed across it. I felt my hand go to my breast pocket almost as if I expected to see the wild faces of the dreaded Shoemans start up spitting lead from one of the dim corners before me. Rushing to the window, I tore down with one sweep of my arm both coat and shawl, and with a start discovered that the window still possessed its draperies in the shape of a pair of discoloured and tattered curtains tied with ribbons that must once have been brilliant and cheery of color.

Nor was this the only sign in the room of a bygone presence that had possessed a taste for something beyond the mere necessities of life.

THE DISAPPEARANCE

On the grim coarsely papered wall hung more than one picture; cut from newspapers.

A bit of candle and a half sheet of a newspaper lay on the floor. I picked up the paper. It was a *Rutland Times* and bore the date of two weeks before. As I read I realized what I had done. If these daring robbers and murderers were not at this very moment in the house, they had been there, and that within a few days.

Stealing cautiously forth from the room, I crept towards the front staircase and listened. All was deathly quiet. The old pine trees moaned and twisted without, and from time to time the wind came sweeping down the chimney with an unearthly shrieking sound that was weirdly in keeping with the place. But within and below all was still as the tomb, and though in no ways reassured, I determined to descend and have the suspense over at once. I did so, pistol in hand and ears stretched to their utmost to catch the slightest rustle, but no sound came to disturb me, nor did I meet on this lower floor the sign of any other presence in the house but my own. Passing hastily through what appeared to be a parlour, I stepped into the kitchen and tried one of the windows. Finding I could easily lift it from the inside, I drew my breath with ease and turning back, deliberately opened the door of the kitchen stove, and looked in. As I half expected, I found a pile of partly charred rags, showing where the wretches had burned their prison clothing, and proceeding further, picked up from the ashes a ring which whether or not they were conscious of having attempted to destroy in this way I cannot say, but which I thankfully put in my pocket against the day it might be required as proof of something, but of what I did not know.

Discerning nothing more of interest, I saw a cellar door but figured it was of no importance, so I gave one look of farewell to the damp and desolate walls about me, then with a breath of relief jumped from the kitchen window again into the light and air of day. As I did so I could swear I heard a door within that old house swing on its hinges and softly close.

My thoughts on the road back, as the old Datsun chugged along, were many and conflicting. Chief above them all, however, rose the comfortable conclusion that in the pursuit of one mysterious affair, I had stumbled, as is often the case, upon the clue to another of yet greater importance, and by so doing got a start that might yet redound greatly to my advantage. For the reward offered for the recapture of the Shoemakers was large, and the possibility of me and Chablis being the one to put the authorities upon their track, certainly appeared after this day's developments, open at least to a very reasonable hope. At all events I determined not to let the grass grow under my feet until I had informed the police of what I had seen and heard that day in the old haunt of two escaped convicts.

Arriving back, I saw that Blake had safely returned there awhile before. I drew the clerk to one side and asked what he could tell me about that old house of the two noted robbers I had passed on my way back among the hills.

"Interesting," he replied, "this is curious. Here I've just been answering the gentleman up stairs a heap of questions concerning that old place, and now you come along with another batch of them; just as if that rickety old den was the only spot of interest we had in these parts."

"Well, I am a man who is always interested in people of an outlaw nature, although these rogues would not top my list of favourite authority questioners. I prefer the Robin Hood types who take from the rich and give to the poor."

"Me, too, my friend, as it appears that all our politicians, except Vermont's Bernie Sanders, prefers to take from the poor and give to the rich. Guess we could call these guys Robin Hoods in reverse."

THE DISAPPEARANCE

"I could think of a lot worse names to call them," I replied. Then, I pressed him again to give me a history of the house and the two thieves who had inhabited it.

"Well," he nonchalantly replied, "ain't much we know about them, yet after all it may be a trifle too much one day. Time was when nobody thought especially ill of them beyond a suspicion or so of their being somewhat mean about money. That was when they kept an inn there, but when the robbery of the Rutland bank was so clearly traced to them, more than one man about here started up and said as how they had always suspected them Shoemans of being villains of the foulest kind. Sent to prison and escaped, and that is the last known of them. A family trait, being a criminal I suppose, as they were all rogues, except the girl."

"And the inn? When was that closed?"

"Just after their arrest."

"Hasn't it been opened since?"

"Only once when a bunch of police came up from Rutland to investigate."

"Who has the key?"

"Ah, I suppose the police now."

I dared not ask how my questions differed from those of Blake, nor indeed touch upon that point in any way. I was chiefly anxious now to return to New York without delay; so paying my bill I thanked the clerk, returned the car and caught the midnight special. By early afternoon I was in Manhattan where I proceeded to carry out my programme by hastening at once to the office and going over things with Chablis and reporting my suspicions regarding the whereabouts of the Shoeman's, suggesting she go to see out friend John Havoc at the 87th Precinct and share the information with him. She did the same that day and I was told that the Vermont authorities had been notified.

That evening I had a talk with Fanny who, to my surprise as a 60 year old man, was outwardly flirting with me and even giving me a nice look at her luscious breasts when she intentionally dropped a fork she was holding and bent over to pick it up in such as a manner that I could see those magnificent orbs. She was bold and forthright when she looked up at me, smiled and said, "I love to have a man fondle them, then spend a long time sucking on the erect nipples which are delightfully tasty." She titillated me so that I reached down and grabbed her, pulling her to me and passionately kissing her as she delightfully sighed in my arms. She whispered, "Come with me sweetheart."

THE DISAPPEARANCE

She led me to a sparsely furnished room off the kitchen with a single bed in it. She wasted no time removing her clothes as I did mine. She purposely did it with her back to me so I could gaze at what is one of the most incredible asses I have ever laid eyes on. She turned around quickly, displaying a magnificent pussy that was delightfully buried in dark hair that surrounded it so completely it was like a dense forest and said, "Take you pick baby, they are all yours and all good."

Now, I am a man who has, in his 60 years, had his share of sex, but let me tell you the 30 minutes we went at it was some of the most incredible sex I have ever had – top five of all time for sure. She led me to the small bathroom off to the left where we showered and took great pains to prepare our sexual organs for the act of love.

She dropped to her knees in the shower and spent time making sure I was ready to pound her with a rock hard tool. She led me to the edge of the bed and whispered, "You can have any hole I got baby. They are all well-used and crave that love tool."

I spent what seemed like hours but was probably no more than 20 minutes pounding first her pussy and then her ass. When I exploded a torrent of love juice in her she acted like I had just deposited all the gold in Fort Knox up her ass. I reached around and put my hand over her mouth to muffle the sound, but she just said, "Baby, they all know I love a good fuck. It is nothing to be ashamed of. This room has seen some great fucks, but you baby just gave me the best I ever had here."

Rolling over exhausted, I looked upon her gorgeous body and realize why I had come to the Blake household in the first place. I said, "Fanny that was the wildest fuck I ever had. Thank you."

She smiled and whispered, "Thank you, and don't make it a one time affair. I know I have good stuff, and it is always here for you when you want it. However, I can see by the look on your face you want to get down to the business that brought you here in the first place. You want to know what I have heard in regards to the disappearance. Such things as I have heard this day!"

"Well," I said, "what? Let me hear too." She put her hand on her heart, covering up the perky nipple which seemed a shame. "I never was so frightened," she whispered. "That elegant lady. Oh my."

"What elegant lady. Don't begin in the middle of your story, I want to hear it all."

"Well," she said, calming down a little, "Ms. Luce had a visitor today, a lady. She was dressed elegantly. Oh what finery she had on."

"O.K., so she was well-dressed, but who was it? Do you know?"

"Her name?" exclaimed Fanny with some sharpness, "how should I know her name; she didn't come to see me."

"How did she look then? You saw her obviously."

"That is what I am telling you. She looked like a queen; as grand a lady as I have ever seen, in her magnificent tailored attire, and her diamonds that were dripping off her."

"Was she a dark woman?" I asked.

"Her hair was as black as the darkest night you could imagine and so were her eyes, if that is what you mean."

"And was she very tall and proud looking?"

Fanny nodded. "You know her?"

"No, not exactly; but I think I can tell who she is. And so she called today on Ms. Luce, did she?"

"Yes, but I guess she knew Mr. Blake would be home before she got away."

"Go on, Fanny."

"It was about three o'clock this afternoon, the time I go up stairs to clean, so I just hung about in the hall a bit, near the parlour door, and I hear her gossiping with Ms. Luce almost as if she was an old friend, and Ms. Luce answering her mighty stiffly and as if she wasn't glad to see her at all. But the lady didn't seem to mind, but went on talking as sweet as honey, and when they came out, you would have thought she loved the woman like a sister to see her look into her face and say something about knowing how busy she was, but that it would give her so much pleasure if she would come some day to see her and talk over old times. But Ms. Luce wasn't pleased a bit and showed plain enough she didn't like the lady. She was going to answer her too, but just then the front door opened and Mr. Blake, with his satchel in his hand, came into the house. And how he did start, to be sure, when he saw them, though he tried to say something polite which she didn't seem to take to at all, for after muttering something about not expecting to see him, she put her hand on the knob and was going right out. But he stopped her and they went into the parlour together while Ms. Luce stood staring after them like a crazy woman, her hand held out with his bag and umbrella in it. She didn't stand so long, though, but came running down the hall, as if she was bewitched. I was dreadful flustered, for though I was hiding behind the wall that juts out there by the back stairs, I was afraid she would see me and shame me before Mr. Blake. But she passed right by and never looked up. There is something dreadful mysterious in this, I thought, and I just made up my mind to stay where I was until Mr. Blake and the lady should come out again from the parlour. I didn't have to wait very long. In a few minutes the door opened and they stepped out, he ahead and she coming after. I thought this was queer as he is always so dreadfully polite in his ways, but I thought it was unusual when I saw him go up the front stairs, she hurrying after, looking I cannot tell you how, but awful troubled and anxious. They went into that room of his he calls his studio and though I knew it might cost me my job if I was found out, I couldn't help following and listening at the keyhole."

Excited, I said, "And what did you hear?"

"Well, the first thing I heard was a cry of pleasure from her, and the words, 'You keep that always before you? You cannot dislike me, then, as much as you pretend.' I don't know what she meant nor what he did, but he stepped across the room and I heard her cry out this time as if she was hurt as well as awful surprised; and he talked and talked, and I couldn't catch a word, he spoke so low; and by and by she sobbed just a little, and I got scared and would have run away but she cried out with a kind of shriek, 'Oh, don't say any more; to think that crime should come into our family. How could you, Tom, how could you.' She sounded so pitiful."

She continued, "Those were the very words she used: 'To think that crime should come into our family! And she called him by his first name, and asked him how he could do it."

"And what did Mr. Blake say?" I retorted a little taken back myself at this result of my efforts with Fanny.

"Oh, I didn't wait to hear as I thought I heard Mr. Blake moving toward the door. I didn't wait for anything. I scurried right downstairs."

"And whom have you told of what you heard in the half dozen hours that have gone by?"

"Nobody."

"Keep it that way," I said as I got up and looked down at that hairy mound. She smiled and spread her legs. I won't bore you Brent with what I did for the next 15 minutes."

CHAPTER 5

THE NEXT REVELATION

Chablis is someone who relates to women well in most cases. The fact she is a transsexual rarely enters the picture. Unless she tells someone, they would never know as her voice and mannerisms are as feminine as any you would ever see; although, when riled up, her ferocity could resemble that of a caged gorilla. I explained to her all that I had uncovered, and I guess somehow I must have even hinted at my dalliance with Fanny, because as we were talking she smiled and said, "Good stuff, old man?"

I brushed it off and asked her what she thought was the best way to approach Mr. Blake's fourth cousin, Evelyn. She reared back in her chair, swivelled a bit to left to right and said, "Got it."

"Got what?"

She tossed a paper from the corner of her desk at me. There was Evelyn Blake's picture in the society section, and she was attending an antique auction as she was a well-known connoisseur of antiques. I nodded my head at Chablis and said, "Yep. Where do I get an antique to get us in to see her?"

Chablis, borrowing a valuable antique from a friend, O.K., from one of her many lovers, would provide the perfect ruse. We went up to Evelyn's suite of 12 rooms at the Waldorf Astoria, which, no doubt, cost at least $25,000 a day and rang the bell. An immaculately attired tall black woman with a British accent greeted us as if we were arrivals from a distant planet. Looking disdainfully at us, she said, "And just what may I do for you two?"

Knowing Chablis, I hoped she could hold her temper and not tell the bitch off. I said, "We have a very rare antique that we believe would be of interest to your mistress."

It came out that Madam was ill and could see no one. I was not, however, to be baffled by one rebuff. Handing the basket I held to the girl, I urged her to take it in and show her mistress what it contained, saying it was a rare article which might never again come her way.

THE DISAPPEARANCE

The girl complied, though with a doubtful shake of the head which was anything but encouraging. Her incredulity, however, must have been speedily rebuked, for she almost immediately returned without the basket, saying Madame would see us.

My first thoughts upon entering the grand lady's presence, was that the girl had been mistaken, for we found her walking the floor in an abstracted way, holding her cell phone in her hand upon which she was obviously reading a text message. She had taken the plaque I had brought, and laid it neglectfully on a nearby table.

But at sight of us standing in the doorway, she hurriedly put the cell-phone on the coffee table and took up the plaque. As she did so, I marked her well and was almost startled at the change I observed in her since that evening with Mr. Blake It was not only that she was dressed in some sort of loose dangling robe that was in eminent contrast to the sweeping silks and satins in which I had hitherto beheld her adorned; or that she was labouring under some physical disability that robbed her dark cheek of the bloom that was its chief charm. The change I observed went deeper than that; it was more as if a light had been extinguished in her countenance. It was the same woman I had beheld standing like a glowing column of will and strength before the melancholy form of Blake, but with the will and strength gone, and with them the glow that danced about her. This was a woman now in complete disarray and totally bewildered by circumstances. What circumstances, of course, I was not sure.

Chablis and I introduced ourselves as just two people who dabbled in antiques. She picked up the plaque and said, "This is a very pretty article you have brought me. Where did it come from, and what recommendations have you to prove it is an honest sale you offer me?"

"None," I said, ignoring with a reassuring smile the first question, "except that I should not be afraid if all the police in New York knew I was here with this fine plaque for sale."

Chablis, eyes taking in everything in the room, was very quiet but offered, "We have no fear of the authorities, I assure you. We came by this item quiet by chance, and I did my research and found out its value."

She gave a shrug of her proud shoulder and softly ran her finger round the edge of the plaque. "I don't need anything more of this kind," said she languidly; "besides," and she set it down with a fretful air, "I am in no mood to buy this afternoon." But then she said, "What are you asking for it?"

THE DISAPPEARANCE

I named an astronomically unfair price. She cast me a startled glance. "You had better take it to some one else; I have no money to throw away."

With a hesitating hand I lifted the plaque. "I would very much like to sell it to you."

Just then a lady's fluttering voice rose from the room beyond inquiring for her, and hurriedly taking the plaque from my hand with an impulsive "Oh there's Amy," she passed into the adjoining room, leaving the door open behind her. I saw a quick interchange of greetings between her and a fashionably dressed lady, and then they withdrew to one side with the ornament I had brought, evidently consulting in regard to its merits. Now was our time. The cell-phone was on the table, still open, and Chablis glanced my way with the look that was waiting for approval, and I nodded affirmatively that she should take a look at the text message. Later, she would share with me what it said:

I have tried in vain to match the sample you sent me at Stewart's, Arnold's and McCreery's. If you still insist upon making up the dress in the way you propose, I will see what Madame Dudevant can do for us, though I cannot but advise you to alter your plans and make the darker shade of velvet do. I went to the Cary

*reception last night and met Lulu Chittenden.
She has actually grown old, but was as lively as
ever. She created a great stir in Paris when she
was there; but a husband who comes home two
o'clock in the morning with blurry eyes and
empty pockets, is not conducive to the
preservation of a woman's beauty. How she
manages to retain her spirits I cannot imagine.
You ask me news of Cousin Tom. I meet him
occasionally and he looks well, but has grown
into the most sombre man you ever saw. In
regard to certain hopes of which you have
sometimes made mention, let me assure you
they are no longer practicable. He has done
what...*

Here the conversation ceased rather abruptly
in the other room, Evelyn made a movement of
advance, and I signalled Chablis to cease and
desist.

Evelyn walked in with a sullen look on her
face and said, "But as I remarked before, I am
not in the buying mood. If you will take half
you mention, I may consider it."

"Pardon us," said Chablis who was ready to
rattle her cage. "We have been considering the
matter and we hold to my original price. There
is someone you know, a cousin, I believe, Mr.
Blake of Washington Square, who may give us
the price we ask if you do not."

THE DISAPPEARANCE

Damn, Chablis was good. Evelyn interjected, "Mr. Blake! Do you sell to him?"

Chablis knew she was on a roll. She said, "We sell to anyone we can, and as he has an artist's eye for such things, well, I think he will pay what we ask."

Her brow furled a bit and she turned away. "I do not want it;" she said, "sell it to whomever you please."

I picked up the plaque from the table and we left the room without another word. Chablis gave me a wink as we left. We had learned more than we expected, but what it meant we were not sure.

Chablis spent the next day doing research on the Shoemans. "Those Shoeman's," she said, "are making a deal of trouble. It seems they escaped the authorities up north and are now somewhere in this city, but where is anybody's guess."

I said, "The coil will tighten."

Contemplatively, Chablis said as she handed me the morning *Times*, "Take a look. I think we are about to have a real wrinkle thrown at us now. I assumed it could end this way, but I hope it wouldn't."

THE DISAPPEARANCE

I took a look at the lower right hand corner where there was a very small article with the headline – *Dead Body Found*:

The dead body of a girl was found in the East River off Fiftieth Street last night. From the appearance she had been dead some time.

That was it! "Come," I said, "let's go and see for ourselves if it should be the one?"

Chablis then let me know news of a dinner party with her reply. "The dinner party proposed by Mr. Blake for tonight may have its interruptions, then."

"Dinner party?"

"Yep," said Chablis as she got up, took my arm and we headed for the morgue.

I do not wish to make my story any longer than is necessary, but I must say that when an hour later, I stood with Chablis before the unconscious form of that poor drowned girl I felt an unusual degree of awe stealing over me: there was so much mystery connected with this affair, and the parties implicated were of such standing and repute in a country where the rich were worshipped by government and the common man as somehow above the fray of we ordinary mortals.

THE DISAPPEARANCE

I almost dreaded to see the covering removed from her face. "A fine looking woman probably," said the morgue attendant.

"Pity the features are not better preserved," offered Chablis as she gazed down upon her.

"No need for us to see the features," I said, pointing to the slightly blonde hair. "The hair is enough; she is not the one." And I turned aside, asking myself if it was relief I felt, because I felt so sorry for Clara and the love she obviously had for Annabelle.

"Damn," I said as I looked again at the prostrate form before me. "Blond hair or black, this is the girl I saw him speaking to that day in the street. I remember her clothes if nothing more." And opening my billfold, I took out the morsel of cloth I had plucked that day that were dropped, lifted up the discoloured rags that hung about the body and compared the two. The pattern, texture and colour were the same.

"Well," said Chablis, pointing to certain contusions, like marks from the blow of some heavy instrument on the head and bared arms of the girl before us; "he will have to answer me one question anyhow, and that is, who this poor creature is who lies here the victim of treachery." And turning to me she said, "There are obvious signs of violence."

I said, "Yes, she has evidently been battered to death."

Chablis' lips closed with grim decision. "A most brutal murder," she said as she softly sighed.

"Well," I said as we slowly walked away from the body, "there is one thing certain. She is not the one who disappeared from Blake's house. So, we are still on the case."

"I am not so sure of that," offered Chablis.

"How?" I said. "You believed Fanny and Clara lied when they gave that description of the missing girl upon which we have gone until now?"

Chablis smiled, and turning her back, beckoned to the official behind us. "Let me have that description that you had from missing persons I see lying there on the table."

The man reached down, took up the official looking paper and handed it to her. She read it and then handed it to me as she said, "I figured there was a missing persons report filed. So, here it is. Read it:"

Look out for the body of a young girl: tall, well shaped and of very fair complexion and a trail of beautiful long black hair.

"I don't understand," I said.

Taking my arm and slightly squeezing, she said, "Next time you examine a room super detective in which anything of a mysterious nature has occurred, look under the bureau and if you find a comb there with several long blond hairs tangled in it, be very sure before you draw any definite conclusions, that the description you received is accurate. I didn't say anything, because I wasn't sure, but she either died her hair, or we have been lied to by more than one person."

I took her by her arm and literally pulled her out of the morgue. She whispered, "Blake's, I assume."

The house maid, not Fanny, greeted us and said when I insisted on seeing Blake, "Mr. Blake is at dinner, sir, with company, but I will call him if you insist."

Wanting to do some thinking, I said, "No, show us into some room where we can be comfortable and we will wait until he has finished."

The servant bowed, and stepping forward down the hall, opened the door of a small and cosy room heavily hung with crimson curtains. "I will let him know that you are here," she said, and vanished towards the dining-room.

Drawing up one of the luxurious arm-chairs to the side of Chablis who had taken a seat on a sofa, I said, "I just wanted to see how rattled he might be. If he is so perplexed that he might curtail his dinner."

Chablis replied, "No, if I am not mistaken we shall find Blake a man of cold, calculating nerve. Not a muscle of his face will show that he is disturbed. The guy is an arrogant asshole, but a cool, calm one."

The next instant a servant stood in the doorway, bearing to our great astonishment, a tray well set with decanter and glasses. "Mr. Blake's compliments," she said, setting it down on the table before us. "He hopes you will make yourselves at home and he will see you as soon as possible."

As I reached for some of the wine, Chablis said, "I think we had better leave his wine alone."

And for half an hour we sat there, the wine untouched between us, listening alternately to the sound of speech-making and laughter that came from the dining-room, and the solemn ticking of the old antique clock as it counted out the seconds on the mantel-piece. Then the guests came in from the dining room, filing before us past the open door on their way to the study for cigars I suppose. They were all gentlemen, well, men anyway. The dinner had been given in honour of a senator, and the character of his guests was in keeping with that of the one thus being complimented.

As they went by us gaily indulging in the jokes and light banter with which such men season a social dinner, I saw Chablis face show that look of disgust she got when she saw pompous assholes playing their game of superiority.

Blake passed us without a word, and they all stayed in the study for what must have been a good 30 minutes. They all slowly departed and some time later, the dignified host advanced with some apology that did nothing to remove the grimace from Chablis' face. I just hoped she could control her tendency to put pompous jerks in their place.

"You have called at a rather inauspicious time, I am afraid," said the Blake, glancing at a card which he held in his hand. "What may your business be tonight may I ask? Something to do with the untimely disappearance I would suppose.

Here it came. Chablis said, "No, jerk-off, we are here to watch a pack of arrogant aristocrats strut about like peacocks."

I surveyed the man in amazement. He simply took it, saying nothing in retort. His face became a bit contorted and he took a deep breath as I said, "I am afraid my partner has a tendency to be rather abrupt sometimes."

He moved toward the door and shut it. Frankly, I was amazed that he took Chablis' sarcasm without rebuke.

"So, you two are interested in some servant girl or other who ran away from this house a week or so ago. Have you found her," he said with a complete lack of concern.

"We think we have," rejoined Chablis with some solemnity. "The river gives up its prey now and then, Mr. Blake."

Still, there was no look of surprise. "Indeed! You do not mean to say she has drowned herself? I am sorry for that, a girl who had once lived in my house. What trouble could she have had to drive her to such an act?"

Chablis moved toward him. "That is what we have come here to learn," she said with a deliberation that bordered on contempt.

THE DISAPPEARANCE

I said, "You who have seen her so lately ought to be able to throw some light upon the subject at least."

"Mr. Adams," he again glanced at the card, "Excuse me, I believe I told you when you were here before that I had almost no dealings with her, or for that matter, none of my servants save Ms. Luce. Therefore, any questions put to me on that subject would be so much labour wasted."

Chablis licked her lips and said, "We are not alluding to any connection you may have had with the girl in this house, but to the conversation you were seen to have with her on a street corner some days ago. You had such a rendezvous did you not?"'"

A flush, deep as it was sudden, swept over Blake's face. "You have me at a disadvantage," he said and stopped. Though a man of intense personal pride, he had but little of that quality called temper, or perhaps if he had, thought it unwise to display it on this occasion. "I saw and spoke to a girl on the corner of a street some days ago, and that she was the one who lived here. I neither knew at the time nor feel willing to believe now without positive proof that it was she?" Then in a deep ringing tone the stateliness of which it would be impossible to describe, he inquired, "Have you presumed to put a spy on my movements, that the fact of my speaking to a poor forsaken creature on the corner of a street should be so notable?"

"Mr. Blake," observed Chablis, and I declare I was never prouder of her, said, "no man who has nothing to hide should be concerned about being followed, unless, of course, he has incurred a suspicion which worries him."

"And do you mean to say that I have been followed," he inquired, clenching his hand and looking steadily at Chablis.

I said, "I have been following you, yes."

Outraged, he riveted his gaze upon me. "In town and out of town?"

I let Chablis reply. "It is known Mr. Blake that you have lately sought to visit the Shoemans."

Blake drew a deep breath, cast his eyes about, let them rest for a moment upon a portrait that graced one side of the wall, and which was I have since learned a picture of his father, and slowly drew forward a chair. "Let me hear what your suspicions are," he said.

I noticed Blake seem to take on a different demeanour as he sighed deeply and sat there staring at both of us like a contrite child ready to be scolded.

"Excuse me," I said, "I do not say I have any suspicions; my errand tonight is simply to notify you of the possible death of the girl Ms. Luce was so concerned about and you were seen to speak with, and to ask whether or not you can give us any information that can aid us in the matter before the coroner."

"If I have been as closely followed as you say, you must know why I spoke to that girl and others, and why I went to the house of the Shoemans. Do you know?" he suddenly inquired.

Neither of us answered as he continued, "You consider you have a right to demand an explanation; let me hear why."

"Well," said Chablis with a change of tone, "I will tell you why Mr. Blake. Imagine yourself a detective hired by a woman to find someone who has disappeared. This woman who hired us, an assistant to a respected citizen, informs us that a girl employed by her has disappeared in a very unaccountable way from her master's house the night before; in fact been abducted as she thinks from certain evidences. Her manner is agitated, her appeal for assistance urgent, though she acknowledges no interest from her employer about the girl's disappearance. She must be found, she declares, and hints that any sum necessary will be forthcoming, though from what source after her own pittance is expended she does not state. When asked if her master has no interest in the matter, she changes color and puts us off. He never noticed his servants, left all such concerns to her, etc.; but shows fear when a proposition is made to consult him. Next imagine yourself with the detectives in that gentleman's house. You enter the girl's room; what is the first thing you observe? Why that it is not only one of the best in the house, but that it is conspicuous for its comforts if not for its elegancies. More than that, that there are books of poetry and history lying around, showing that the woman who inhabited it was above her station; a fact, which others are presently brought to acknowledge. You notice also that the wild surmise of her abduction by means of the window and French doors has some ground in appearance, though the fact that she went with entire unwillingness is not made so apparent. Your assistant insists in a way that indicating some special knowledge of the girl's character or circumstances that she never went without compulsion; a statement which the torn curtains and the track of blood found, would seem to emphasize. In fact, let us go to that room now and I think I can tell you how she was made to bleed."

THE DISAPPEARANCE

Nodding his acquiescence, we stepped upstairs and Chablis went over to the desk. She picked up the letter opener and said, "My guess is this instrument was wiped clean of blood and that the laboratory will find the blood that was wiped away will match that of the girl who disappeared from here if we find her."

She went on: "A few other facts are made known. My guess is this instrument was used by the girl to ward off her enemies. Its frail and dainty character proves indisputably that it was employed by the girl herself, and that against manifest enemies; no man being likely to snatch up any such puny weapon for the purpose either of offence or defence. That these enemies were two and were both men was insisted upon by Ms. Luce who overheard their voices."

Now, she was really moving along rapidly. "Mr. Blake, such facts as these arouse curiosity, especially when the master of the house being introduced upon the scene, fails to manifest common human interest, while his assistant betrays in every involuntary gesture and expression she makes use of, her horror if not her fear of his presence, and her relief at his departure. Curiosity sir begets inquiry, and inquiry elucidated further facts such as these, that the mysterious master of the house was in his garden at the hour of the girl's departure, was even looking through the bars of his gate when she, having evidently escaped from her captors, came back with every apparent desire to re-enter her home, but seeing him, betrayed an unreasonable amount of fear and fled back even into the very arms of the men she had endeavoured to avoid. Do you to speak sir?" asked Chablis suddenly stopping, with a sly look at his left shoe.

Mr. Blake shook his head. "No,"

"Inquiry revealed, also, two or three other interesting facts. First, that this gentleman qualified though he was to shine in ladies' society, never obtruded himself there, but employed his leisure time instead in walking the lower streets of the city, where he was seen more than once conversing with certain poor girls at street corners and in blind alleys. The last one he talked with believed from her characteristics to be the same as the woman who was abducted from his house."

"Hold there," said Mr. Blake with some authority in his tone, "there you are mistaken; that is impossible."

"Ah, and why," said confident Chablis who was reeling with pleasure over me allowing her to continue the inquisition unimpeded by my commentary.

"The girl you allude to had brighter hair, something which the woman who lived in my house did not possess."

"Indeed. I thought you had never noticed the woman who worked here, sir, did not know how she looked?"

"I should have noticed her if she had had such hair as the girl you speak of."

Chablis smiled and opened her pocketbook. "There is a sample of her hair Mr. Blake that I cut off her when the morgue attendant turned to talk to Aaron," she said, taking out a thin strand of brilliant hair and showing it to Blake. "Bright you see, as that of the unfortunate creature you talked with the other night."

She then walked over to the desk and picked up the comb, removing some hair from it. "This hair and that may match up I am sure. Maybe coloured by Miss Clairol or some other brand, but it could match in DNA, believe me."

Arrogantly, stiffing his demeanour and puffing out his chest, he said, "We waste our time," as he looked directly at Chablis. "All that you have said does not account for your presence here or the tone you have used while addressing me. What are you keeping back? I am not a man to be trifled with."

THE DISAPPEARANCE

Chablis took a seat as a sign of indifference to his admonitions. Damn I thought, I taught that girl well. "You are right," she said, glancing briefly in my direction. "All that I have said would not perhaps justify me in this intrusion, if.." she looked again towards me. "Do you wish me to continue," she asked.

Mr. Blake's intent look deepened. "I see no reason why you should not utter the whole amount of rubbish. A good story loses nothing by being told to the end. You wish to say something about my journey to the Shoeman's house, I suppose."

"I am just starting, Mr. Blake. Just getting warmed up."

"Then," said Mr. Blake, "it is no longer necessary for us to prolong this interview. I have allowed, nay encouraged you to state in the plainest terms what it was you had or imagined you had against me, knowing that my actions of late, seen by those who did not possess the key to them, must have seemed a little peculiar. But when you say you have no interest in any mystery disconnected with the girl who has lived in my house, I can with assurance say that it is time we quit this unprofitable conversation, as nothing which I have lately done, said or thought here or elsewhere has in any way had even the remotest bearing upon that individual; she having been a stranger to me while in my house, and quite forgotten by me, after her unaccountable departure hence."

"You deny then," Chablis said, "all connection between yourself and the woman who occupied this room."

"I am not in the habit of repeating my assertions," said Mr. Blake with some severity, "even when they relate to a less disagreeable matter than the one under discussion."

Chablis very carefully looked over at me and I winked. She took the cue and said lying, "I am sorry I have too much respect for the man I believed you to be when I entered this house earlier to go with the thing unsaid which is lying at present like a dead weight upon my lips. I dare not leave you to the consequence of my silence; for duty will compel me to speak some day and in some presence where you may not have the opportunity which you can have here, to explain yourself with satisfaction. Mr. Blake I cannot believe you when you say the girl who lived in this house was a stranger to you."

Mr. Blake drew his proud form up in a disdain that was only held in check by the very evident honesty of Chablis. "You are courageous at least," he said. "I regret you are not equally discriminating."

"Pardon me," said a contrite sounding Chablis, "I would like to justify myself before I go. Not with words," she proceeded as the other folded his arms with a sarcastic unconcern. "I am done with words; action accomplishes the rest. Mr. Blake, I believe you consider me an honest woman though perhaps lacking in the social graces. Will you accompany me to your private room for a moment? There is something there which may convince you I was neither playing the fool nor acting with too much bravado."

I expected to hear the haughty master of the house refuse a request so peculiar. But he only bowed, though in a surprised way that showed his curiosity was aroused by this incredible woman I was privileged to call my partner. "My room is at your disposal," he said, "but you will find nothing there to justify your assertions."

"Let me at least make the effort," entreated Chablis, who looked over at me, knowing I was enjoying watching my protégé perform so brilliantly.

Mr. Blake, frowning bitterly, immediately led the way to the door. There was in Chablis' face a smug recognition that she was performing brilliantly.

"Now ma'am," said Mr. Blake, turning upon her with a stern expression, "the room and its contents are before you; what have you to say for yourself."

Chablis, equally stern, and extremely composed, cast one of her inscrutable glances round the apartment and without a word stepped before the picture hanging on the wall.

I thought Mr. Blake looked surprised, but his face was not one that lightly expressed emotion. "A portrait of my cousin," he said with a certain dryness of tone.

"Fourth cousin, I believe," said Chablis.

"Yes."

"Fourth cousins can marry in this state."

Blake bowed his head as in thought, but did not answer to Chablis' statement of fact. For a moment he stood looking with a strange lack of interest at the proudly brilliant face of the painting before him.

Then Chablis stepped forward and with a quick gesture turned the picture rapidly to the wall and even I was amazed that I had overlooked that important clue. Before us from the reverse side of that painted canvas was no luxurious brunette countenance now, steeped in pride and languor, but a face, let me see if I can describe it. But no, it was one of those faces that are indescribable. You draw your breath as you view it; you feel as if you had had an electric shock; but as for knowing ten minutes later whether the eyes that so enthralled you were blue or black, or the locks that clustered halo-like about a forehead almost awful in its expression of weird, unfathomable power, were brown or red, you could not nor would you pretend to say. It was the character of the countenance itself that impressed you. You did not even know if this woman who might have been anything wonderful or grand was truly beautiful or not. You did not care; it was as if you had been gazing on a tranquil evening sky and a lightning flash had suddenly startled you. Is the lightning beautiful? Who asks! But I know from what presently transpired that the face was ivory pale in complexion, the eyes deeply dark, and the hair, strange and uncanny in combination, of a peculiar bright dark hue.

"You dare!" came forth in strange broken tones from Mr. Blake's lips.

I instantly turned towards him. He was gazing with a look that was half indignant, half menacing at the silent detective who with eyes drooped and finger directed towards the picture, seemed to be waiting for him to finish.

"I do not understand an audacity that allows you to, to…" his voice trailed off and you could almost sense he was about to cry.

"I declared my desire to justify myself," said Chablis. "I had no idea before I turned the picture for sure what was there. I only suspected. This is my justification. Do you note the color of the woman's hair whose portrait hangs with its face turned to the wall? Is it like or unlike that of the strand I showed you?"

Blake moved a trifle aback as Chablis said, "Just observe the dress in which this woman is painted; blue silk you see, dark and rich; a wide collar cunningly executed, you can almost trace the pattern; a brooch; then the roses in the hand, do you see? Now come with me back downstairs."

Too much startled to speak, Mr. Blake, haughty aristocrat as he was, turned like a little child and followed us. Once there, Chablis said, "You accuse me of insulting you, when I express disbelief of your assertion that there was no connection between you and the girl Annabelle," said Chablis as she opened the desk drawer. "Will you do so any longer in face of these?" And drawing off the towel that lay uppermost, she revealed the neatly folded dress, wide collar, brooch and faded roses that lay beneath. "Ms. Luce assures us these articles belonged to her; were brought here by her. Dare you say they are not the ones reproduced in the portrait in your room?"

Mr. Blake uttering a cry sank on his knees before the drawer. "Oh no, Oh no," was his only reply, "what are these?" Suddenly he rose with his whole form quivering, his eyes filled with tears. "Where is Ms. Luce?" he cried, hastily advancing and pulling a bell cord "I must see her at once. Send Ms. Luce here," he ordered as Fanny smiling demurely made her appearance at the door.

"Ms. Luce is out," returned the girl, "went out as soon as you got up from dinner, sir."

"Gone out at this hour?"

"Yes sir; she goes out very often nowadays, sir."

Blake frowned. "Send her to me as soon as she returns," he commanded, and dismissed the girl.

"I don't know what to make of this," he now said in a strange tone, approaching again the touching contents of that open desk drawer with a look in which longing and doubt seemed in some way to be strangely commingled. "I cannot explain the presence of these articles in this room; but if you will come back upstairs I will see what I can do to make other matters intelligible to you. Disagreeable as it is for me to take anyone into my confidence; affairs have gone much, much too far for me to hope any longer to preserve secrecy as to my private concerns."

We made our way upstairs and, for some reason, Chablis reached over and took my hand, squeezing it. She looked at me, then at Blake for the first time in a sympathetic way.

He moved not in his usual brisk manner, but slowly, shoulders stooped over as if he had the weight of the world on them. I hated having sympathy for rich people who seemed to always think the world was supposed to bow and scrape before them. Ever since I had seen the arrogance of the Bush family that seemed to think they were somehow entitled, I had never been able to reconcile wealth with sympathy for those who appeared haughty and arrogant as they did.

I could see Chablis was now feeling sympathy for Blake, and she was worse than I was when it came to disdain for the rich. She moved up beside him as we reached the top of the stairs. The two of them went into the studio, and the next revelation was about to begin.

CHAPTER 6

DESERVED SO MUCH BETTER

Blake, as he entered the studio, said, "you have presumed, and not without reason I should say, to infer that the original of the portrait and the woman who has so long occupied my house, are one and the same. You will no longer retain that opinion when I inform you that the reverse picture," he remarked as he pointed at it, "strange as it may appear to you, is the likeness of my wife."

"Wife!" We both were astonished as I take it, but it was my voice which spoke. "We were ignorant you ever had a wife."

"No doubt," continued our host smiling bitterly, "that at least has evaded the knowledge of most." Then with suddenly found courteous manner, he continued "She was never acknowledged by me as my wife, nor have we ever lived together, but if priestly benediction can make a man and woman one, that woman as you see her there is my lawful wife."

Rising, he softly turned the lovely, potent face back to the wall, leaving us once more confronted by the dark and glowing countenance of his cousin.

"I am not called upon," he said, "to go any further with you than this. I have told you what no man until this hour has ever heard from my lips, and it should serve to exonerate me from any unjust suspicions you may have entertained. But to one of my temperament, secret scandal and the gossip it engenders is only less painful than open notoriety. If I leave the subject here, a thousand conjectures will at once seize upon you, and my name if not hers will become, before I know it, the football of gossip if not of worse and deeper suspicion than has yet assailed me."

He sighed deeply and continued, "I take you to be honest in your way and guarded of your own reputation and that of those with whom you are connected. If I succeed in convincing you that my movements of late have been totally disconnected with the girl whose cause you profess solely to be interested in, may I assume you will keep silent?"

THE DISAPPEARANCE

"You may count upon our discretion as regards all matters that do not come under the scope of fiduciary duty as we cannot be accessories after the fact. You understand," I said to him.

"I do, yes."

And, perhaps for the first time in his life he was forced to reveal his inner nature, as he began his story in these words:

"Difficult as it is for me to introduce into a relation like this the name of my father; I shall be obliged to do so in order to make my conduct at a momentous crisis of my life intelligible to you. My father, back then, was a man of strong will and a few but determined prejudices. Resolved that I should sustain the reputation of the family for wealth and respectability, he gave me to understand from my earliest years, that as long as I preserved my manhood from reproach, I had only to make my wishes known, to have them immediately gratified; while if I crossed his will either by indulging in dissipation or engaging in pursuits unworthy of my name, I no longer need expect the favour of his countenance or the assistance of his purse."

He took in a deep breath. "When, therefore, at a certain period of my life, I found that the charms of my cousin Evelyn were making rather too strong an impression upon my fancy for a secured peace of mind, I first inquired how such a union would affect my father, and learning that it would be in direct opposition to his views, cast about in my mind what I should do to overcome my passion. Travel suggested itself, and I took a trip to Europe. But the sight of new faces only awakened in me comparisons anything but detrimental to the beauty of her who was at that time my standard of feminine loveliness. Nature and the sports connected with a wild life were my next resort. I went to California, roamed the mountains of Colorado, and probed the wildernesses of Canada and our Northern states. It was during these last excursions that an event occurred which has exercised the most material influence upon my fate, though at the time it seemed to me no more than a trivial matter."

Again he sighed and continued. "I had just returned from Canada and was resting in tolerable enjoyment of a very beautiful autumn in the Adirondacks when a letter reached me from a friend then in the vicinity of where he was urging me to join him in a certain small town in Vermont where we could do some fishing."

"Being in a somewhat reckless mood I at once wrote a consent, and before another day

was over, started for the remote village whence his letter was postmarked – Bellow Falls. I found it by no means easy of access. Situated in the midst of hills some thirty kilometres or so distant from the railroad station, I discovered that in order to reach it, a long ride was necessary, followed by a somewhat shorter journey on foot. Not being acquainted with the route, I timed my connections wrong, so that when evening came I found myself in a rental car riding over a strange road in the darkest night I had ever known. As if this was not enough, my car gave trouble and the motor completely stopped. It was therefore with no ordinary satisfaction that I presently beheld a lighted building in the distance, which as I approached resolved it to be an inn. Stopping in front of the house, which was closed against the chill night air, I called out lustily for someone to allow me entrance, whereupon the door opened and a man appeared on the threshold. I at once made my wishes known, receiving in turn a somewhat gruff acquiescence to my need for shelter."

"I entered the house. Another man met me on the threshold who merely pointed over his shoulder to a lighted room in his rear. I at once accepted his silent invitation and stepped into the room before me. Instantly I found myself confronted by the rather startling vision of a young girl of a unique and haunting style of

beauty, who rising at my approach now stood with her eyes on my face and her hands resting on the card table before which she had been sitting, in an attitude expressive of mingled surprise and alarm. To see a woman in that place was not so strange; but such a woman! Even in the first casual glance I gave her, I at once acknowledged to myself her extraordinary power. Not the slightness of her form, the pallor of her countenance, or the fairness of the locks of light dark hair that fell in two long braids over her bosom, could for a moment counteract the effect of her dark glance or the vivid almost unearthly force of her expression. It was as if you saw a flame starting before you, waving tremulously here and there, but burning and resistless in its white heat. I was awe-struck to say the least."

"A shudder passed over her, but she made no effort to return my acknowledgement. As we cast our eyes dilating with horror, down some horrible pit in the corner of the room. She allowed her gaze for a moment to dwell upon my face, then with a sudden lifting of her hand, pointed towards the door as if to bid me depart, when it swung open with that shrill rushing of wind that involuntarily awakes a shudder within you, and the two men entered and came stamping up to my side. Instantly her hand sunk, not feebly as with fear, but calmly as if at the bidding of her will, and without waiting for

them to speak, she turned away and quietly left the room. As the door closed after her, I noticed that she wore a see through, sheer nightgown."

"The older of the two men told the other to go after Laura and tell her to make up the bed in the northwest room."

"The elder man, a large powerfully framed fellow, frowned. It was an evil frown, and the younger one seemed to feel it. He immediately tossed his coat onto a chair and left the room to go after Laura,"

He made a comment about boys are so disobedient now-a-days, saying they should be broke in and do as they are told and asked no questions.

"I smiled to myself at his calling the broad shouldered, strapping six-footer who had just left us a boy, but merely asked if he was his son as I took a seat in front of the crackling fire to warm myself. He replied the scrapping youth was indeed his son, and that girl I saw was his daughter."

"Now, the place I actually wanted to go was called Bentonville, so I asked how far it was and he said only a short distance, but it was not a journey to make at night, as the road was very

winding and treacherous.

"He glanced down at my baggage which consisted of a small hand bag, an over-coat and a fishing pole, with something like a gleam of disappointment as he suggested I stay the night, which I said I could not so as my friend was expecting me."

"His hand went to his beard in a thoughtful attitude and he cast me what, with my increased experience of the world, I should now consider a sinister glance and asked if I was expected by my friend."

"I quickly told him yes that I was expected as I stretched out my feet in front of the fire. He asked if I had been on the road long and we engaged in some meaningless small talk. Well, I assumed it was meaningless anyway."

"He drew a chair up to my side, a proceeding that was interrupted, however, by the re-entrance of his son, who without any apology crowded into the other side of the fire-place in a way to sandwich me between them. Not fancying this arrangement which I, however, imputed to ignorance, I drew back and asked if my room was ready. It seemed it was not, and unpleasantly as it promised, I felt forced to reseat myself and join in, if not support, the conversation that followed. So,

THE DISAPPEARANCE

follow me closely here, as this is where things begin to become clearer."

Blake took a deep breath and continued. "A half hour passed away, during which the wind increased until it almost amounted to a gale. Spurts of rain dashed against the windows with a sharp crackling sound that suggested hail, while every sound of distant thunder, rumbled away among the hills in a long and reverberating peal that made me feel glad to be housed even under the roof of these rude and uncongenial creatures. Then, suddenly the conversation turned upon the time and time-pieces, when in a low even tone I heard that my room was ready. Turning my head, I saw standing in the doorway the slight figure of the young girl whose appearance had previously so impressed me. I got up and was told by the elder gentleman not to be concerned about the creaks and cracklings all over the house as the place was very old and had many nuances one finds in such a place."

"The young lady took me upstairs into a large clumsily furnished room whose enormous canopy bed draped with heavy curtains looked rather imposing.

"I thanked her and said goodnight at which she at once departed with a look of still determination upon her countenance that I

found it hard to explain. Left alone in that large, bare and dimly lighted room, with the wind shrieking in the chimney and the powerful limbs of some huge tree beating against the walls with a heavy thud inexpressibly mournful, I found to my surprise and something like dismay, that the sleepiness which had hitherto oppressed me, had in some unaccountable way entirely fled. In vain I contemplated the bed, comfortable enough now in its appearance that the stifling curtains were withdrawn; no temptation to invade it came to arouse me from the chair into which I had thrown myself."

"It was as if I felt myself under the spell of some invisible influence. I remember turning my head towards a certain quarter of the wall as if I half expected to encounter there the bewildering glance of a serpent. Yet far from being apprehensive of any danger, I only wondered over the weakness of mind that made such fancies possible."

"I drew off my coat, unloosened my vest and was about to throw it off, when I realized my wallet was in it. Going to the door in some unconscious impulse of precaution I suppose, I locked myself in, and then drawing out my wallet, took from it a roll of bills which I put into a small side pocket, returning the wallet to its old place. I threw my vest onto the chair in the far corner and sat back down."

THE DISAPPEARANCE

"Why I did this I can scarcely say. As I have before intimated, I was under no special apprehension. I was at that time anything but a suspicious man, and the manner and appearance of the men below struck me as unpleasantly disagreeable but nothing more than that coursed through my mind. But I not only did what I have related, but allowed the light to remain on for some reason, lying down finally in my clothes."

"How long I lay listening to the creaking and groaning of the rickety old house, I cannot say, nor how long I remained in the doze which finally seized me, as I became accustomed to the sounds around and over me. Enough that before the storm had passed its height, I awoke as if a hand touched me in the dark, and leaping with a bound out of the bed, beheld to my incredible amazement, the alert, nervous form of the girl who was named Laura standing before me. She had my coat in her hand, and it was her touch that had evidently awakened me. She was staring at me intently and said that it would be wise for me to get out. She whispered for me to follow her, and I did."

"The wind became so fierce that I thought the house would be swept from its foundation. She said it was too fearful a night for me to be out alone and that she would go with me. She helped me gather up my stuff and as we started

to go down the stairs we both heard something at the bottom. She said it was her father and brother and that they would tell me it was folly to leave on such a night, but that the only real safety for me was out trudging along that stormy highway."

"She bounded down the stairs with me, pushed open a door at the bottom, and stepped at once into the room we had left an hour or so before. There was, in that room, an ominous chill as of distinct peril that coursed through my veins. Nothing at first sight seemed to be a reason, but I felt it nonetheless. The fire which had not been allowed to die out, still burned brightly on the hearthstone, but it was not that which awakened my apprehension. Nor was it the loud ticking clock on the mantel-piece with its hand pointing silently to the hour of eleven. Nor the heavy quiet of the scantily-furnished room but it was the sight of those two powerful men drawn up in grim silence, the one against the door leading to the front hall, the other against that opening into the kitchen."

"A glance at Laura standing silent and undismayed at my side, however, instantly reassured me. With that will exercised in my favour, I could not but win through whatever it was that menaced me. Slinging my bag over my shoulder, I made a move towards the door and the silent figure of my host. But with a quick

outreaching of her hand, she drew me back and told me to stand still as she insisted her brother, whom she called Carl, who stood sullen, but less menacing like than his father, to allow me to pass and leave the house so that I might be able to reach the person whom I sought."

"She told her rugged-looking brother that she did not ask many favours, but that she was pleading with him to let me go. He quickly told her that I would be a fool to go out into such a miserable night and that he could not allow such a foolish endeavour. She, however, kept insisting as she took my hand and moved toward him. All the while the father, to the other side stood in silence, but she finally turned to him and asked if he would let me go? He very defiantly said the door was locked and would stay that way."

"Still she wilfully pleaded as I stood in abject silence. Her father quickly bounded from the door where he stood and was striding hastily towards her. In my apprehension I put up my arm for a shield, for he looked ready to murder her, but I let it drop again as l caught her glance which was like white flame undisturbed by the least breeze of personal terror. She pointed down at the floor and told him he would stop and stop now. She said to him that one more step and that for which he

would sell his soul would be tossed in the fire. Drawing from her breast a huge roll of bills, she stretched them out as she moved to the fire."

"Threatening to throw those bills in the fire brought the father to an immediate halt. She told him she was not a girl of many words, but those words were meant with earnest. Suddenly, the younger of the two made a rush as he left his post and in another instant would have had his powerful arms about her slender form, only that I met him half way with a blow that laid him on the floor at her feet. She said nothing, but one of the bills immediately left her hand and fluttered into the fire where it instantly shrivelled into nothing. With the yell of a mad beast wounded in his most vulnerable spot, the old man before us stamped with his heel upon the floor, begging her to stop. He moved to the door and unbolted it saying that she could leave but to please leave the money."

"She insisted he step aside, which he did and we left into the stormy night. The older man was standing at the open door with pleading eyes. She told him she would bring the money back upon her return and we stepped off the porch."

"The blast of driving rain struck our faces and enveloped us in a cloud of wet, as that

slender girl grasped my hand and drew me away through the blinding darkness. It was not that I was so much affected by her beauty as influenced by her power and energy. The fury of the gale seemed to bend to her will, and the wind lent wings to her feet. Arriving at the roadside, she paused and looked back. The two burly forms of the men we had left behind us were standing in the door of the inn; in another moment they had plunged forth and towards us. With a low cry the young girl leaped towards a tree where she whispered we would wait. Unseen behind the tree, her brother and father rushed by us with grim determination into the storm."

"She again took me by the hand, and we hurried away as she said I should trust her and she would get me to shelter. Her hand tightened on mine, and we hastened on as speedily as the wind and rain would allow. After a short but determined breasting of the storm, during which my breath had nearly failed me, she suddenly stopped and said she had to be careful as we were near a steep and dreadful precipice that runs near where we were."

"There was something in her manner that awakened a chill in my veins almost as if she had pointed out some dreadful doom which I had unwittingly escaped as we tread an obviously dangerous path. How far we

travelled through the mud and tangled grasses of that horrible path I do not know. It seemed a long distance. At last she paused. When looking up I saw that we were in front of a small cottage."

"No refuge ever appeared more welcome to a pair of sinking wanderers I am sure. Wet to the skin, dabbled with mud, exhausted from the punishing gale, we stood for a moment under the porch to regain our breath, then with her characteristic energy she lifted the knocker and struck a smart blow on the door. In a few moments we were standing once more before a comfortable fire hastily built by the worthy couple whose slumbers we had thus interrupted. As I began to realize the sweetness of conscious safety, all that this young, heroic creature had done for me swept warmly across my mind. Looking up from the fire that was beginning to infuse its heat through body, I surveyed her as she slowly undid her long braids and shook them dry over the blaze, and almost started to see how young she was. Not more than eighteen I should say, and yet what an invincible will shone from her dark eyes and dignified her slender form; a will gentle as it was strong, elevated as it was unbending. I bowed my head as I watched her, in grateful thankfulness which I presently put into words that actually seemed to affect her deeply as she realized just how thankful I was."

THE DISAPPEARANCE

"As the couple prepared us hot drinks, she said that she simply did the duty of a person who cared about another and she said if I was indeed grateful I should never, under any circumstances tell anyone what had happened that fateful night at the inn, especially about the money."

"Instantly I remembered a suspicion which had crossed my mind while there at that infernal house, and my hand went almost involuntarily to my vest pocket. The roll of bills was gone. I drew out my empty hand, looked at it, but said nothing as she said that I had lost nothing because the money was not as important as my life and that I should leave it at that. I did."

"She explained that they had often taken money and that she saw no need to risk injury over such that I had, so she was going to give it to them if I acquiesced. She explained that they saw me take out money through a hole pierced in the wall of the room I occupied, and the sight made them mad. They were going to kill me and then toss me over the precipice below there. But she overheard them talking and so she hurried up to my room to wake me as she had to take possession of the bills for my own safety. She took them quietly because she hoped to save me without betraying them. But she failed in that. She asked me to please

understand as regardless they were her father and brother."

"*I explained to her that the money was trivial, and that I would never betray her. At that moment I looked into her eyes and saw such beauty of mind, heart and body. I knew this was an extraordinary woman.*"

"*She smiled at me so serenely. It was a wintry gleam but it ineffably softened her face. I became conscious of a movement of pity towards her as I said to her that I was sorry she had such a hard lot in life. However, she simply said she was born to it and it was her destiny, but that it was not her destiny to be a criminal. Then, she very calmly told me that she would never go back to that abominable house again, only arrange to send them the money.*"

"*She retired to a bedroom and I slept on the sofa. The following morning I stumbled upon her sitting in the kitchen reading a book by Hemingway, and all of a sudden impulse seized me and I asked her if she would like to be educated. The instantaneous illumining of her whole face was sufficient reply without the emphatic words that followed. It is not necessary for me to relate with what pleasure I caught at the idea that here a chance to repay in some slight measure the inestimable favour she had done me; nor by what arguments I finally won her to accept an education at my hands as some sort of recompense for the life she had saved. The advantage which it would give her in her struggle with the world she seemed duly to appreciate, but that so great a favour could be shown her without causing me much trouble and an unwarrantable expense, she could not at once be brought to comprehend, and until she could, she held out with that gentle but inflexible will of hers. The battle, however, was won at last and I left her in that little cottage, with the understanding that as soon as the matter could be arranged, she was to enter a certain university in upstate New York with the head-master of which I was acquainted. Meanwhile I managed to get her a job with a friend in Boston until as such time as she could start school."*

Needless to say my dear Brent, by this time we were beginning to look upon Mr. Blake in a different light. True, he might still be pompous, but, obviously, there was some innate goodness within him, and I noticed that Chablis was looking at him in a different light also. Her eyes were focused on him now and she was following every word very closely as he continued.

"I was a careless fellow in those days but I kept my promise to that girl. I not only entered

her into that school for a course of four years, but acting through its master, who had taken a great fancy to her, supplied her with the necessities her position required. It was so easy; merely the signing of a check from time to time and it was done. I say this because I really think if it had involved any personal sacrifice on my part, even of an hour of my time, or the labour of a thought, I should not have done it, as I am sure the two of you have deduced that I am a bit self-absorbed."

At that point, Chablis interjected, "A bit?"

He laughed and continued his tale. *"For with my return to the city my interest in my cousin revived, absorbing me to such an extent that any matter disconnected with her soon lost all charm for me. The years passed; I was the slave of Evelyn Blake, but there was no engagement between the two of us. My father's determined opposition was enough to prevent that. But there was an understanding which I fondly hoped would one day open for me the way of happiness. But I did not know my father. Sick as he was—he was at that time labouring under the disease which in a couple of months later bore him to the tomb. He kept an eye upon my movements and seemed to probe my inmost heart. At last he came to a definite decision and spoke, saying that I was his only child, as he remarked, and it had been and was the desire of his heart to leave me as rich and independent a man as himself. But I seemed disposed to commit one of those acts against which he had the most determined prejudice; marriage between cousins being in his eyes an unsanctified and dangerous proceeding, liable to consequences the most unhappy. If I persisted, he must will his property elsewhere. The Blake estate should never descend with the seal of his approbation to a race of probable imbeciles. So, he not only robbed me of the woman I loved, but with a clear insight into the future, I presume, insisted upon my marrying someone else of respectability and worth before he died. Obviously, my love of money and position precluded my love of Evelyn. I am sure you find that disgusting, and frankly so do I, as it shows what a weakling I am."*

I saw in Chablis that look of sympathy that so frequently imbedded itself on her face. She was now beginning to see Blake in a different light, beginning to understand why he acted the way he did, beginning to develop empathy for a man who was flawed as a result of a domineering father to whom he simply did not have the will to disobey. As he continued, I saw the sympathy building in her heart.

"The idea of me marrying someone other than Evelyn, had seized upon him with great force, and I soon saw he was not to be shaken

out of it. To all my objections he returned with but one demand – that I marry within three months, as he knew his time was drawing near. He said that within that time if I did not bring someone suitable before him that he must look around for an heir who will not thwart his dying wishes. Thus, much to my dismay, I sat out to find someone to satisfy his whim."

"I surveyed the fashionable belles that nightly thronged the parlours of my friends and felt my heart sink within me. Take one of them for my wife, loving another woman? Impossible. Women like these demanded something in return for the honour they conferred upon a man by marrying him. Wealth? They had it. Position? That was theirs also. Consideration? Ah, what consideration had I to give? I turned from them with distaste. My cousin Evelyn gave me no help. She was a proud woman and loved my money and my expectations as much as she did me. She said if I had to marry to maintain my wealth, then I should do so, but she insisted that my wife must be a plainer and a less aspiring woman than she. Then, upon my father's death, she said I could quietly divorce, give the poor wretch a stipend and marry her."

"I must admit that I became a bit disillusioned with her callousness, but my love for her was still there. Meanwhile the days flew

by. If my own conscience had allowed me to forget the fact, my father's eagerly inquiring, but sternly unrelenting gaze as I came each evening to his bedside, would have kept it sufficiently in my mind. I began to feel like one in the power of some huge crushing machine that was gradually pressing the life out of me, but my love of money, power and position was disgustingly driving me onward."

"How or when the thought of Laura as a wife first crossed my mind I cannot say. At first I recoiled at the idea and put it away in disdain; but it ever recurred and with it so many arguments in her favour that before long I found myself regarding it as a refuge. To be sure she was beneath my station in so many ways, but she seemed to be the kind of wife demanded of me. She was allied to rogues if not villains, I knew; but then had she not cut all connection with them, dropped away from them, planted her feet on new ground which they would never invade? I commenced to cherish the idea. With this friendless, grateful, unassuming protégée of mine for a wife, I would be as little bound as might be. She would ask nothing, and I need give nothing, beyond a home and the common attentions required of a gentleman and a friend. I should have a fair wife and an obedient one, but no vulgarized shadow of Evelyn, thank God, or of any of her fashionably dressed friends. Of course, the

question was could I fool my father into accepting her as a suitable replacement?"

"Advanced thus far towards the end, I went to see Laura. I had not beheld her since the morning we parted at the door of that little cottage in Vermont, and her presence caused me a shock. This, the humble waif with the appealing grateful eyes I had expected to encounter? This tall and slender creature with dark but lightened hair about a face that was as magnificent as any I had ever seen! I felt a half movement of anger as I surveyed her. What beauty! I was so taken aback; I lost all the condensations I had intended to infuse into her. She seemed to feel my embarrassment and a half smile fluttered to her lips. That smile decided me. It was sweet but above all else it was appealing. How I won that woman to marry me in ten days time I care not to state. Not by holding up my wealth and position before her. Something restrained me from that. I was resolved, and perhaps it was the only point of light in my conduct at that time, not to buy this young girl. I never spoke of my expectations, I never alluded to my present advantages yet I won her. We were married, there, in the quietest and most unpretending manner. Why the fact has never transpired I cannot say. I certainly took no special pains to conceal it at the time, though I acknowledge that after our separation I did resort to such *measures as I thought necessary, to suppress what had become a thorn in my pride. My first move after the ceremony was to bring her immediately to New York and to this house. With perhaps a pardonable bitterness of spirit, I had refrained from any notification of my intentions, and it was as strangers might enter an unprepared dwelling, that we stepped across the threshold of this house and passed immediately to my father's room."*

"I can give you no wedding and no honeymoon I had told her as my father is dying and demands my care. From the altar to a death bed may be sad but it is an inevitable condition of her marriage to me. And she had accepted her fate with a deep unspeakable smile it has taken me long months of loneliness and suffering to understand."

"I shall never forget how my father roused himself in his bed, nor with what eager eyes he read her young face and surveyed her slight form swaying towards him in her sudden emotion like a flame in a breeze. Nor while I live shall I lose sight of the spasm of uncontrollable joy with which he lifted his aged arms towards her, nor the look with which she sprang from my side and nestled, yes nestled, on the breast that never to my remembrance had opened itself to me even in the years of my earliest childhood. For my father was a stern

man who believed in holding love at arm's length and measured affection by the depth of awe it inspired. He proclaimed her his daughter, and she proclaimed she had never had a father. It is impossible for me to continue without revealing depths of pride and bitterness in my own nature, from which I now shrink with unspeakable pain. So far from being touched by this scene, I felt myself grow hard under it. If he had been disappointed in my choice, queried at it or even been simply pleased at my obedience, I might have accepted the wife I had won, and been tolerably grateful. But to love her, admire her, glory in her when Evelyn Blake had never succeeded in winning a glance from his eyes was almost unbearable. I could not endure it; my whole being rebelled, and a movement like hate took possession of me. Bidding my wife to leave me with my father alone, I scarcely waited for the door to close upon the poor young thing before I told him that I had brought him a daughter as commanded, but that I could not live with a woman I did not love."

Tom Blake shifted in his seat, sighed deeply and one almost sensed he was ready to cry. But he continued:

"Instantly, and before my lips could move, the door opened and the woman I thus repudiated in the first dawning hour of her

young bliss, stood before us. What a face! When I think of it now, when from dreams that gloomy as they are, beset me in my waking hours, I see from the surrounding shadows that young fair brow with its halo of hair, blotted, by the agony that turned her that instant into stone, I wonder I did not take out the pistol that lay in the table near which I stood, and shoot her lifeless on the spot as some sort of a compensation for the misery I had caused her as she overheard what I said."

"Straight as a dart, but with a disconsolate look of hurt on her face, she came towards us and asked if indeed I married her because I was commanded to do so? She bowed her head and cried. I saw my father's stiff and pallid lips move silently as though he would answer for me if he could, and summoning up what courage I possessed, I told her that I deeply regretted she had overheard my inconsiderate words. I told her that I had never meant to wound her, whatever bitterness lay in my heart towards one who had thwarted me in my dearest and most cherished hopes. That I humbly begged her pardon and would so far acknowledge her claim upon me as to promise that I would leave my home at this time, if it distressed her; my desire being not to injure her. She, through tears, said that she had loved me so, since that time at the inn. My father barked that I should not rob him of such a fine

daughter. She said that she could not remain with a man who looked upon her with contempt. She said that she loved me so much that she would give me back the freedom I had squandered With a gesture that was like a benediction, she turned, and noiselessly, breathlessly as a dream that vanishes, left the room."

"I heard a cry come from my father's lips. I saw he had fainted. I could not leave him so. Calling to Ms. Luce, who was never far from my father in those days, I bade her stop the lady. I believe I called her my wife, who was going down the stairs, and then rushed to his side. It took minutes to revive him. When he came to, it was to ask for the creature who had flashed like a beacon of light upon his darkening path. I rose as if to fetch her but before I could advance I heard a voice say, 'She is not here,' and looking up I saw Ms. Luce glide into the room. That was the last time I was privileged to gaze upon a woman who deserved so much better than Thomas Hewett Blake."

CHAPTER 7

RIGOROUS EFFORT

We all are guilty of judging people without walking in their shoes. At that moment, Chablis and I had not altered our feelings that Blake was a pompous ass in so many ways, but we also had sympathy for him now, and realized that much of his arrogance was inherited and the result of circumstances over which he had no control.

Chablis, now more cordial, asked how long his father lived after the incident. He replied, "My father, who had received in this scene a great shock, began to fail so rapidly. He demanded my constant care; and though from time to time as I ministered to him and noted with what a yearning persistency he would eye the door and then turn and meet my gaze with a look I could not understand, I caught myself asking whether I had done a deed destined to hang forever about me like a pall; it was not till after his death that the despairing image of the bright young creature to whom I had given my name, returned with any startling distinctness to my mind, or that I allowed myself to ask whether the heavy gloom which I now felt settling upon me was owing to the sense of shame that overpowered me at the remembrance of the past, or to the possible loss I had sustained in the departure of my young unloved bride."

I said, "And what of Evelyn Blake?"

"The announcement of the engagement between Evelyn and the Count De Mirac happened soon after my father's death. Though I had never in the most passionate hours of my love for her lost sight of that side of her nature which demanded as her right the luxury of great wealth; and though in my tacit abandonment of her and secret marriage with another I had certainly lost the right to complain of her actions whatever they might be, this manifest surrendering of herself to the power of wealth and show at the price of all that women are believed to hold dear, was an undoubted blow to my pride and the confidence I had unconsciously reposed in her inherent womanliness and affection. That she had but made on a more conspicuous scale, the same sacrifice as myself to the god of wealth and position, was in my eyes at that time, no palliation of her conduct. Still, I constantly had visions of Laura that preyed so heavily upon my mind. I recalled that Laura had told me that she loved me so dearly that when the day came that I needed her all I should do was cry out. Ah, but my pride. I longed to forget I was held by a tie that known to the world would cause me the bitterest shame. For by this time the true character of her father and brother had been revealed and I found myself bound to the daughter of a convicted criminal. But I could not forget her. The look with which she had left me was branded into my consciousness. Night and day it floated before me, till to escape it I resolved to fasten it upon canvas, if by that means I might succeed in eliminating it from my dreams. The painting you have seen is the result. Born with an artist's touch and insight that under other circumstances might, perhaps, have raised me into the cold dry atmosphere of fame, the execution of this piece of work, presented but few difficulties to my somewhat accustomed hand. Day by day her beauty grew beneath my brush, startling me often with its spiritual force and significance until my mind grew feverish over its work, and I could scarcely refrain from rising at night to give a touch here or there to the floating hair or the piercing, tender eyes turned, ah, ever turned upon the inmost citadel of my heart with that look that slew my father before his time and made me, yes me, old in spirit even in the ardent years of my first manhood. At last it was finished and she stood before me life-like and real in the very garments and with almost the very aspect of that never to be forgotten moment. Even the roses which in the secret uneasiness of my conscience I had put in her hand when she departed with me for this very home, as a sort of visible token that I regarded her as my bride, and which through all her interaction with my father she had never dropped, blossomed before me on the canvas. Nothing that could give reality to the likeness was lacking; the vision of my dreams stood embodied in my sight, and I looked for peace. Alas, that picture now became my dream. It haunted me."

Chablis leaned forward and said, "And putting it behind Evelyn's portrait was a way of hiding it from the view of others, but my guess is that you turned it around almost daily, and that was why you kept to yourself in that room."

"Inserting it behind that portrait of Evelyn, which had held its place above my armchair, I turned its face to the wall when I rose in the morning, but at night it beamed ever upon me, becoming as the months passed, the one thing to hold to and muse over when the world grew a little noisy in my ears and the never ceasing conflict of the ages beat a trifle too loudly on heart and brain. Meanwhile, I heard no word of her, only of her villainous father and brother; no token that she had escaped evil or was removed from want. If I had loved her I could have succoured her, but I did not know where to find her. Her countenance illuminated my wall, but her fair young self lay for all I knew sheltered within the darkness and silence of the tomb."

I said, "So, your melancholia made you boorish and you lost any interest in the goings on here in this house."

"Yes, at length my morbid broodings worked out their natural result. A dull melancholy settled upon me which nothing could break. Even the news that my cousin, who had lost her husband so soon after marriage, had returned to America with expectation to remain, scarcely caused a ripple in my apathy. Was I still in love with Evelyn or had my passion dampened?"

"So," said Chablis, "you sought her out?"

"Yes, and seeking her where I knew she would be found, I gazed again upon her beauty. It was absolutely nothing to me. A fair young face with high thoughts in every glance floated like sunshine between us and I left the haughty countess, with the knowledge burned deep into my brain, that the love I had was now slain for her but was alive and demanding for my darling young wife. I loved Laura not Evelyn. Laura whom I had tossed away was the passion of my life."

Chablis, always outwardly seemingly more interested in sex than love, I could tell was beginning to soften toward Blake, as she, like most women, genuinely believed in the power of love to draw two people of radically different backgrounds together.

Blake, his guard now down, let his emotions flow and he shared his innermost thoughts. "Once assured I no longer loved Evelyn, my apathy vanished like mist before a kindled torch. Henceforth the future held a hope, and life a purpose. I would seek my wife throughout the world and bring her back, even if I found her in prison between the men whose existence was a curse to my pride. But where should I turn my steps? What golden thread had she left in my hand by which to trace her through the labyrinth of this world? I could think of but one and that was the love which would restrain her from going away from me too far. The Laura of old would not leave the city where her husband lived. If she was not changed, I ought to be able to find her somewhere within this great Babylon of ours.

THE DISAPPEARANCE

Wisdom told me to set the police upon her track, but pride bade me try every other means first. So with the feverish energy of one leading a forlorn hope, I began to pace the streets if haply I might see her face shine upon me from the crowd of passers by; a foolish fancy, unproductive of result! I not only failed to see her, but anyone like her. You followed me in my determined quest for solace, Mr. Adams. I knew you were there. Did you not think it queer that I never had a dalliance with any of those ladies?"

"I did. Yes, I did."

"In the midst of the despair occasioned by this failure a thought flashed across me or rather a remembrance. One night not long since, being uncommonly restless, I had risen from my bed, dressed and gone out into the yard back of my house for a little air. It was an unusual thing for me to do but I seemed to be suffocating where I was, and nothing else would satisfy me. As you already surmise, it was the night on which Annabelle disappeared of which you have so often spoken, but I knew nothing of that, my thoughts were far from my own home and its concerns. You may judge what a state of mind I was in when I tell you that I even thought at one moment while I paused before the gate leading into the street that I saw the face of her with whom my thoughts were ever busy, peering upon me through the bars."

"Now, you tell me that I did see a girl there, and that it was Annabelle; it may be so, but at the time I considered it a vision of my wife, and the remembrance of it, coming as it did after my repeated failures to encounter her in the street, worked a change in my plans. For regard it as weakness or not, the recollection that the vision I had seen wore the garments of a working-woman rather than a lady, acted upon me like a warning not to search for her any longer among the resorts of the well-dressed, but in the regions of poverty which abound here in this great city where they are the by-product of a cruel economic system. I therefore took to wanderings such as I have no heart to describe. Nor do I need to, if, as you have informed me, I have been followed almost continuously. I knew you were there, or at least sensed it, many times, and now, of course, I know you were usually there."

I said, "I can understand now most of your actions, but why, knowing you truly love Laura, did you seek out Annabelle that night?"

"The result of my plight was almost madness. Though deep in my heart I felt a steadfast trust in the purity of Laura's intentions when she left, the fear of what she might have been driven to by the awful poverty and despair I every day saw seething about me, was like hot steel in brain and heart. Then her father and her brother! To what might they not have forced her, innocent and loving soul though she was! Drinking the cup of despair as I had never considered it possible for me to taste, I got so far as to believe that her eyes would yet flash upon me from beneath some of the tattered shawls I saw sullying the forms of the young girls upon which I hourly stumbled. Yes and even made a move to see my cousin, if haply I could so win upon her compassion as to gain her consent to shelter the poor creature of my dreams in case the necessity came and Laura refused to return to my arms. But my heart failed me at the sight of her cold face above the splendour she had bought with her charms, and I was saved a humiliation of asking, but I would now endure any humiliation if I just knew dear Laura was truly safe."

"Next day I started for the rambling old house in Vermont as you know, if haply in the spot where I first saw her, I might come upon some clue to her present whereabouts. But the old inn was deserted, and whatever hope I may have had in that direction perished."

Chablis said, "But what of the contents in that bureau drawer in Annabelle's room?"

"I can say nothing. If, as I scarcely dare to hope, they should prove to have been indeed brought here by the girl who has since disappeared so strangely, who knows but what in those folded garments a clue is given which will lead me at last to the knowledge for which I would now barter all I possess in this world that is now so sullen to me."

At that moment, he got up, walked over to the pull cord and summoned Ms. Luce. Surprised were we all when an immaculately attired Clara walked. "You want me, sir," said Clara, marble faced with a look of fear imbedded in her eyes.

"Yes," murmured Blake. "Ms. Luce, I want a direct and honest answer. Who, who really was that girl you harboured in that room below for so long? Speak; what was her real name and where did she come from?"

Trembling in every limb, she cast a desperate look at us as Blake became more demanding. "Tell us Ms. Luce, now!"

"Oh," she said, sinking into a chair from sheer inability to stand as result of psychological exhaustion, "it was your wife, Mr. Blake, the young creature you."

"What?"

THE DISAPPEARANCE

All the agony, the hopelessness, the love, the passion of those last few months flashed up in that word. She stopped as if she had been shot, but seeing the hand which he had hurriedly raised, fall slowly before him, Clara began to cry.

She went on with a burst of emotion. "Oh sir, she made me swear on my knees I would never betray her, no matter what happened. To my shame, I blackmailed her into having sex with me to keep her secret. When not two weeks after your father died she came to the house and asking for me, told me all her story and all her love; how she could not reconcile it with her idea of a wife's duty to live under any other roof than that of her husband, and lifting off the black wig which she wore, showed me how altered she had made herself by that simple change—in her case more marked by the fact that her eyes were in keeping with black hair, while with her own brighter locks they always gave you a shock as of something strange and haunting. I gave up my will as if forced by a magnetic power, and not only opened the house to her but my heart as well; swearing to all she demanded and keeping my oath too, but I fell so deeply in love that I betrayed her to my lust. She acquiesced to my desires, but I always knew it was you she loved, only giving me what I wanted to make sure I kept her secret. I have been despicable."

"I care nothing of your sordid lustfulness. I only care for her and what she endured to just be near me. How it must have hurt her that I ignored her so, not even knowing she was in my house. How repulsive she had to cater to your desires to be near me."

Bowing her head, she said, "I am so sorry sir."

Seemingly unconcerned with her apology, he said, "Despicable. Despicable!"

"Ah," returned the agitated woman, "Do you not think I suffered? To be held by my oath, an oath I was satisfied she would wish kept even at this crisis, yet knowing all the while she was drifting away into some evil that you, if you knew who she was, would give your life to avert from your honour if not from her innocent head! To see you cold, indifferent, absorbed in other things, while she, who would have perished any day for your happiness, was losing her life perhaps in the clutches of those horrible villains! Do not ask me to tell you what I have suffered since she went; I can never tell you, innocent, tender, noble-hearted creature that she was."

"Was?" His hand clutched his heart as if it had been seized by a deathly spasm. "Why do you say was?"

THE DISAPPEARANCE

Chablis and I knew what was coming now, but we could not alter the hurt that was about to be hurled upon him, so we sat silent.

"Because I have just come from the Morgue where she lies dead on a stiff slab in that abominable place."

"No," came in a low shriek from his lips, "that is not she; that is another woman, like her perhaps, but not she. It cannot be!"

"No sir, it is she minus her wig. Such hair as hers I never saw on anyone before. I wish it were I laying there, not her."

Just then a revelation came to me. I was not 100% sure it was Laura on that slab in the morgue. Chablis looked at me with blazing eyes, as she too, obviously from her demeanour, had her doubts. "Mr. Blake is right," I broke in. "The woman taken out of the East River has been both seen and spoken to by him. Now, I remember her on the street. He spent great deal of time talking to her, even walking along side her for a distance. He should know if it is his wife. It is not. It was the woman I followed after you parted from her. I remember now, did Laura have a mole below her left ear, as does the girl in the morgue."

"No," he empathically replied.

I smiled and said, "Not her then."

The assurance seemed to lift a leaden weight from her heart. "Oh thank God," she murmured bowing her head and sobbing. Then with a sudden return of her old tremble, "But I was only to reveal her secret in case of her death! What have I done? Oh what have I done? Her only hope lay in my vow to keep her secret."

Mr. Blake leaning heavily on the table before him looked in her face. "Your blackmailing her for sex is despicable. I should fire you on the spot."

"Yes sir," she said in sorrow.

He took a deep breath and said, "No, no, I love her too, and I think you do also. I cannot chastise you for love, only for the blackmailing to satisfy your lust. We shall see if we can move on from this. I shall not dismiss you. However, should she be unforgiving if I am lucky enough to find her, it will be her decision what must be done with you."

She leaped to her feet with a joyous bound. "You love her? Oh thank God! I love her too, but so much that I am relieved that you love her, because that is all she desires in life – your love." Weeping with unrestrained joy, she sat there just sobbing.

THE DISAPPEARANCE

Of course after that, all that remained for us to do was to lay our heads together and consult as to the best method of renewing our search after the unhappy girl, now rendered of double interest to us by the facts with which we had just been made acquainted. That she had been forced away from the roof that sheltered her by the power of her father and brother was of course no longer open to doubt. They were the two who took her. To discover them, therefore, meant to recover her. The capture of those despicable cretins became the leading purpose of our two lives? We told Clara that she was no longer obligated to pay us.

Blake quickly interjected. "I shall pay you whatever your fee is, and if this poor woman has advanced you any money, give it back to her and I will make restitution for the same. You are now in my employ, if you would do me the honour."

Chablis was too quick to allow me to answer as she joyfully said, "It will be an honour to work for you Mr. Blake."

I nodded my head in agreement and we got up, preparing to leave. Blake walked over to Clara, reached down and helped her rise from the chair. He wrapped his arms around her and said, "Working for me and my father could not be a pleasant endeavour. You have endured much, and I know that you crave love and affection, but do not find it among those in this household. I shall try to be a more model employer in the future, but do not expect miracles."

Chablis and I looked at each other and smiled. Blake noticed, and said to us, "I know I appear to be an abominable person, and have made your job more difficult. I shall also try to be more amenable to you also."

Chablis walked over to him and put her arm around him, giving him a warm hug and saying, "You have endured much heartache in a search for that which is ever elusive – love. We will forgive you being such an asshole!"

We all laughed and together we prepared to tackle the disappearance of Annabelle, sans Laura, together in a defined and rigorous effort.

CHAPTER 8

A MOST PERPLEXING CASE

Next morning Chablis and I met in serious consultation. We ask ourselves how, and in what direction should we extend the inquiries necessary to a discovery of the Shoemakers and perhaps locate Laura?

Chablis said, "They are German. Should we go to the Germantown section of Manhattan?"

"No," I said. "They are too smart for that. They would not hide in an ethnic enclave. You must remember they are not alone, but have with them a young woman of a somewhat distinguished appearance, whose presence in a crowded district, like that, would be sure to awaken gossip; something which, above all else, they must want to avoid. This will not be easy."

"If they dared to ill-treat her, it would be different. But she is a valuable piece of property to them you see, a choice lot of goods which it is for their interest to preserve in first-class condition until the day comes for its disposal. They took her to extort money from Mr. Blake, so she is valuable to them."

Chablis was just thinking out loud now. "What they want is too keep close so they can make their move easily. So, they are close by, but where?"

"Well, they have hampered themselves with this woman at this time for the purpose of using her hereafter in a scheme of black-mail upon Mr. Blake. He, then, must be the object about which their thoughts revolve and toward which whatever operations or plans they may be engaged upon must tend. What follows? When a company of men have made up their minds to rob a bank, what is the first thing they do? They hire, if possible, a house next to the special building they intend to enter and for months work upon the secret passage through which they hope to reach the safe and its contents; or they make friends with the watchman who guards its treasures, and the janitor who opens and shuts the doors. In short they hang about their prey before they pounce upon it. And so will these Shoemakers do in the somewhat different robbery which they plan sooner or later to effect. Whatever may keep them close at this moment, Mr. Blake and Mr. Blake's house is the point toward which their eyes are turned - pretty simple for a skilled detective like yours truly."

"I would recommend a little bait about Mr. Blake's house," said Chablis, "for, if as you say, they are nearby, those men are already within eye-shot of the prey they intend to run down."

"But," I said. "I have been living myself in that very neighbourhood and know by this time the ways of every house in the vicinity. There is not a spot up and down the street for ten blocks where they could hide away for two days much less two weeks, and as for the side streets, why I could tell you the names of those who live in each house for a considerable distance. In this respect, I am thoroughly perplexed. I have been in the area and may have overlooked something. You take a look with a fresh perspective and see what you find."

And what success Chablis had, and by what means did she attain it? By that of the simplest, prettiest clue ever, a clue so simple a child would have seen it. But let me explain: when after a wearisome day spent in an ineffectual search through the neighbourhood, a tired

Chablis went home to her apartment, where on the way up, she ran into Cordell Bloomquist. Now, it is well-known by all that Chablis is a woman who has a tickle that must often be scratched by a man with a large tool. Well, as they were going up the elevator, she looked over at Bloomquist and said, "Cordell, I know you have wanted to get some of this fine stuff for a long time. I don't know whether it is my womanly charms or just your prurient interest in a transsexual, but I am tired of those lustful glances that you are too timid to follow up on. You want to fuck me, come out and say it. You might get lucky."

Cordell actually began to shake, so taken aback was he by Chablis' direct approach to the courting game. He stuttered, "I,I,I…"

Smiling, Chablis moved toward him as the elevator came to a halt at her floor. She was close enough that he could feel her breath. "Stop stuttering – can it big boy. You want it or not?"

"O.K., this was Cordell's first sex with a transsexual, so I know that you are a conservative sort Brent; consequently, I shall not go into great detail about the sex."

"Oh, come on. You don't introduce the titillation and then stop."

"Well, O.K., then. Actually, it does hold a key to the case, so maybe it appropriate I tell you about the escapade."

Chablis is not a woman who is ashamed of her sexuality. She walked across the threshold of her apartment, immediately turned and embraced Cordell in a long, passionate kiss, their tongues dancing a delightful tune of lust. She led him to the shower and said, as she undressed except for her panties. "Are you ready Cordell? If you think it may be too much of a shock, I can leave them on. I am very good at hiding it, if it offends you."

"No Chablis. I am ready, but I can't touch it. I hope you understand."

"I do, of course. It is pretty useless anyway," she said as she slowly removed her panties. He looked out of curiosity, but then moved to her, embracing and passionately kissing those succulent lips. In the shower the two engaged in much touching, fondling and kissing. The excitement was so palpable that one could almost cut it with a knife.

Leading him to bed, she gently laid him down, crawled on top of him and began to moan as their lips met in the ecstasy of the moment, their bodies entwined in blissfulness as they floated into a sea of tranquil lust.

THE DISAPPEARANCE

Chablis slowly worked her way toward the root of his passion, pausing along the way to kiss and nibble, prolonging the anticipation of what Cordell knew would be the absolute greatest blow job he had ever had. Finally arriving at the pubic hair, she gently nestled her face in it, blew on it and began to knead his balls gently with her right hand. His erection was massive, and it was all Chablis could do to keep from devouring it immediately, as she longed to savour its taste and the feel of it in her warm mouth. Still controlling her desires as she knew it would be better if she waited patiently for him to get so excited that he would begin to pump, pump vigorously as she sucked. Oh, how she loved to excite a man with her mouth, making him become overwhelmed with desire.

Finally, Cordell began to beg. "Please Chablis. Please."

Now she had accomplished what she wanted. It was then that she very adroitly moved above his massive tool, blew on the tip, slowly opened her mouth and breathed her hot breath upon it before she swiftly took it all in and swallowed it completely all the way to the base, her nose buried in his pubic hair. Back and forth, back and forth she feverously worked as if her very life depended upon coaxing that delightful white liquid from Cordell's tool.

Cordell moaned and groaned with delight. This was a woman whose mouth could be sold as a vacuum cleaner, as she seemed to be sucking the very soul out of him. Ironically, Chablis was probably enjoying it more than he was, as the sense of power it gave her was often overwhelming. She could feel the joy juice beginning to fight for release, but she would slow down each time he got ready to blow and he would let out a mournful sigh. Then she decided the delay was more than he could stand. In one mighty thrust downward and then an incredible pull backward, he exploded like a box of TNT, slamming his hot liquid down her throat.

Exhausted, all he could utter was, "Chablis, Chablis………."

She crawled up on him and said as she looked into his eyes, "My pleasure Cordell, my pleasure entirely."

Now, I will not go into more detail on their fornicating, as it went on for another two hours, but after all the pleasure-taking was over, they lay there in blissfulness, and Cordell said something that made Chablis realize just why Aaron may have been unable to find Laura. He looked at her as she lay in his arms and said, "You know Chablis, sometimes what you really want is right there in plain sight."

Chablis looked at him and said, "Say that again."

"What you really want is right there in plain sight. I live two doors down from you, and just didn't realize that what I really needed was right there down the hallway."

A light went on in Chablis' head and she said, "Thanks, you may have just given me the answer to a perplexing puzzle. We will do this again soon I hope, but I really have to go now. Thanks to you, I'm about to make an important move in solving a case."

As previously stated, Aaron had taken a room across the street from the Blake home to keep an eye on him. Chablis figured that might be the key. There was an old saying "hide in plain sight." Aaron couldn't find Annabelle (Laura) because she was perhaps in plain sight.

Chablis got Aaron's key to the place he had across from Blake's and told him she would check back in a few hours, explaining that it was her theory that since the place was a rooming house, why would the Shoemakers not perhaps have taken a room there. Chablis tried to find the landlady, but she did not answer her buzz, so she went inside and began a methodical sojourn down the hallways, knocking on various doors.

THE DISAPPEARANCE

Finally, she went to the third floor and without any suspicion of the fact, tried the door of the room directly over Aaron's. No answer, so she stepped back and her foot trod upon something that broke under her weight. She never let even small things pass without some notice. Stooping then, for what she had thus inadvertently crushed, she picked it up and carried it toward the window for better light. Examining the object, she found it to be a piece of red chalk. What was there in that simple fact awoke a train of thought that would lead to the two desperate thieves?"

She called me and I was there in a flash. She showed me what she had found. She remembered a very abstract thing I had mentioned about seeing a red cross scrawled on the panel of one of the doors in that old house. It seemed a trivial thing at the time and made little or no impression upon either of us. But remembered now, it was of great significance.

Full in the centre of the wall to the left, we beheld distinctly scrawled, probably with the very piece of chalk Chablis held, a small red cross precisely similar in outline to the one I had seen a few days before on the panel of the Shoemaker's' door. What the hell a red cross meant, neither of us was certain, but the discovery sent a thrill over us that almost raised our hair on end. Was, then, this famous trio to be found in the very house in which I had been living for a week or more? I could not withdraw my gaze from the mysterious looking object Chablis held. I bent near the door, I listened, I heard what sounded like the suppressed snore of a powerful man, and almost had to lay hold of myself to prevent my hand from pushing open that closed door and my feet from entering. As it was I did finger the knob a little, but an extra loud snore from within reminded me by its suggestion of strength that discretion was the better part of valour.

I therefore withdrew, but for the whole night Chablis and I lay awake downstairs listening to catch any sounds that might come from above, and going so far as to plan what we would do if it should be proved that it was indeed the men from Vermont.

With the breaking of day upon us, a rude step was heard going up the stairs a few minutes before and we followed. But I presently considered that my wisest course would be to sound the landlady and learn if possible with what sort of characters I had to deal with. Routing her out of the kitchen, where at that early hour she was already engaged in domestic duties, we drew her into a retired corner and put our questions. She was not backward in replying. She had conceived an innocent liking for me in the short time I had been with her and was only too ready to pour out her griefs into my sympathizing ear. For those men were a grief to her, acceptable as was the money they were careful to provide her with. They were not only almost always in the house, one of them, smoked his old pipe constantly and blackened up the walls, and they both looked so shabby, and kept the nice girl so close, and if they did go out, came in at such unheard of hours. It was enough to drive her crazy; yet the money, the money as always was the key factor.

I grew a bit weary waiting for what I wanted hear from her, so I said, "But the girl? What of the girl?"

"So nice, so quiet, so sick-looking! I cannot stand it to see her cooped up in that small room always watched over by one or both of those burly wretches. The old man says she is his daughter and she does not deny it, but oh my a wonderful girl coming from the seed of that brute."

It was obvious that money was an inducement for this woman, and the astute Chablis interjected, "If she is who we believe she is, there well may be a very handsome, very substantial reward from a wealthy interested party."

THE DISAPPEARANCE

Her eyes lit up like two beacons on a dark night. So, without further disguise I acquainted the startled woman before me with the fact that I was not, as she had always considered, the clerk out of employment whose daily business it was to sally forth in quest of a situation, but one Aaron Adams, private detective and the lovely lady with me was the well-known Chablis Louise Chavez.

She was duly impressed and easily persuaded to second all my operations as far as her poor wits would allow, giving me free range of her upper story, and above all, promising that secrecy without which all my finely laid plans for capturing the rogues without raising a scandal, would fall headlong to the ground.

By noon of that same day, I was domiciled in an apartment next to the one whose wall by his door bore that scarlet sign which had aroused within us such feverish hopes the night before. Clad in the seedy garments of a broken down artist whose acquaintance I had once made, with something of his air and general appearance and with a few of his wretched daubs hung about on the whitewashed wall, I commenced with every prospect of success as I thought, that quiet espionage of the hall and its inhabitants which I considered necessary to a proper attainment of the end I had in view.

THE DISAPPEARANCE

A hacking cough was one of the peculiarities of my friend, and determined to assume the character in total, I allowed myself to startle the silence now and then with a series of gasps and choking sounds that whether agreeable or not, certainly were of a character to show that I had no desire to conceal my presence from those I had come among. Indeed it was my desire to acquaint them as fully and as soon as possible with the fact of their having a neighbour: a weak-eyed half-alive innocent to be sure, but yet a neighbour who would keep his door open night and day and went rambling about through the hall speaking to those he met and expecting a civil word in return.

As I expected, I had scarcely given way to three separate fits of coughing, when the door next me opened with a jerk and a rough voice called out, "Who's that making all that noise?"

A soft voice interrupted him and he drew back. "I will go see," said those gentle tones, and Laura, for I knew it was she before the skirt of her robe had advanced beyond the door, stepped out into the hall.

I was yet bent over my work when she paused before me. The fact is I did not dare look up; the moment was one of such importance to me. I did not need to see her, I felt her, as if she were a fresh breeze of hope.

"You have a dreadful cough," she said with a tinge of true sympathy in her voice that goes unconsciously to the heart. "Is there something I can do for you, something I might get you to relieve the cough?"

I pushed back my work, drew my hand over my eyes, and glanced up. "No, I am sorry if it disturbs you. It is a chronic condition. Almost like a chronic condition of the heart of one who loves and believes no love comes in return."

She threw back the shawl which she had held drawn tightly over her head, and advanced with an easy gliding step close to my side. "What a strange thing to say, but true it is. Loving someone and not being loved in return is as debilitating as any disease. You do not disturb me, but my father is a trifle cross sometimes, and if he should speak up a little harsh now and then, you must not mind. I am sorry you are so ill."

What is there in some women's look, some women's touch that more than all beauty goes to the heart and subdues it? As she stood there before me in her dark beauty with long locks flowing gently over her shoulders, her whole person undignified by art and un-graced by ornament, she seemed just by the power of her expression and the fineness of her manner, the loveliest woman I had ever beheld.

THE DISAPPEARANCE

"You are very kind," I murmured, half ashamed of my disguise as deceiving her seemed a crime within itself, though there was purpose to what I was doing. "Your sympathy goes to my heart." Then as a deep growl of impatience rose from the room at my side, I motioned her to go and not irritate the man who seemed to have such control over her.

"In a minute," she said, "first tell me what you are painting."

So I told her and in the course of telling, let drop such other facts about my fancied life as I wished to have known to her and through her to her father. She looked sweetly interested and more than once turned upon me that dark eye, of which I had heard so much, full of tears that were as much for me, scamp that I was, as for her own secret trouble. But the growls becoming more and more impatient she speedily turned to go, repeating, however, as she did so, "Now remember what I say, you are not to be troubled if they do speak cross to you. They make noise enough themselves sometimes, as you will doubtless be assured of tonight."

And the lips which seemed to have grown stiff and cold with her misery, actually softened into something like a smile. Oh, that smile lit up my room as my heart hurt for her pain.

THE DISAPPEARANCE

She looked so sweet, so tender, so saintly as she tilted her head and started to walk away. The nod which I gave her in return had the solemnity of a vow in it. I was going to protect her at all costs.

My mind thus assured as to the correctness of my suspicions, and the way thus paved to the carrying out of my plans, I allowed a day to elapse without further action on my part. My motive was to acquaint myself as fully as possible with the habits and ways of these two desperate men, before making the attempt to capture them upon which so many interests hung. For while I felt it would be highly creditable to my sagacity, as well as valuable to my reputation as a detective, to restore these escaped convicts in any way possible into the hands of justice, my chief ambition after all was to so manage the affair as to save the wife of Mr. Blake, not only from the consequences of the despair caused by these two, but from the publicity and scandal attendant upon the open arrest of two heavily armed men. Strategy, therefore, rather than force was to be employed, and strategy to be successful must be founded upon the most thorough knowledge of the matter with which one has to deal. Chablis was growing impatient and wanting to tell Blake. I pleaded with her to wait so that we could get things wrapped up free of any encumbrance. She agreed.

THE DISAPPEARANCE

Three days, then, did I give to the acquiring of knowledge, the result of which was the possession of the following facts:

1. That the landlady was right when she told me the girl was never left alone, one of the men, if not the father then the son, always remaining with her.

2. That while thus guarded, Laura was not imperturbably restricted as she had the liberty of walking in the hall, though never for any length of time.

3. That the cross by the door seemed to possess some secret meaning connected with their presence in the house; it having been erased one evening when the whole three went out on some matter or other, only to be chalked on again when in an hour or so later, father and daughter returned alone.

4. That it was the father and not the son who made most purchases as were needed, while it was the son and not the father who carried on whatever operations they had on hand; nightfall being the favourite hour for the one and midnight for the other; though it not infrequently happened that the latter sauntered out for a short time also in the afternoon, probably for the drink he could not go long without.

5. That they were men of great strength but little innate intelligence.

How best to use these facts in the building up of a matured plan of action, was, then, the problem. By noon of a certain day I believed it to have been solved, and reluctant as I was to leave the spot of my espionage even for the hour or two necessary to a visit Chablis at the office, I found myself compelled to do so.

Laura appeared at my door as I was preparing to leave. She asked how my cough was to which I replied that it had gotten better.

"Come back here," shouted a heavy voice from the room she had left. "Leave that coughing fool alone and get back here."

A smile went through me as I looked upon her with great pity and she said, "My father is in one of his impatient moods. I should go. You have a nice day."

"What is that," were words bellowed as I head thundering footsteps. "What are you two up to?"

"Go, as I see you are leaving," she said "and try to get something for that cough." And she moved gently toward the door like an angel in flight to bring mercy to the sick.

THE DISAPPEARANCE

"When I return," I was forced to pause in my words, as the elder Shoemaker, having by this time reached the open doorway where he stood frowning in upon us in a way that made my heart stand still for her.

"What are you two talking about?" he said; "and what have you got in your case there?" he continued with a stride forward that shook the floor, but stopped and then walked out.

He laid one heavy hand upon her slight shoulder and led her from the room. It was all I could do to keep from crushing the miscreant bastard into rubble on the floor.

I waited no longer than was necessary to carry my feeble and faltering steps appropriately down the stairs, to reach the floor below and gain the landlady's presence.

I was in constant anxiety during my absence; an absence necessarily prolonged as I had to stop and explain matters to Chablis, who was anxious to join me in the final act of this sordid affair.

"Well," she said after I had informed her of the discoveries I had made, "I saw Tom Blake this morning and I tell you we will find him a grateful man if this affair can be resolved satisfactorily."

"That is good," I said, "gratitude is worth more than money."

Then she said, "Perhaps it is no more than our duty to let him know that his wife is safe and under our eye; though I would by no means advocate his knowing just how near him she is, until the moment comes when he is wanted, or we shall have a lover's impetuosity to deal with as well as all the rest." Then with a hurried remembrance of a possible contingency, went on to say, "But, I also worry about Clara Luce, who is, without doubt, every bit as much in love with Clara as Blake."

"She is indeed, and this is a matter for the three of them to straighten out not us, but I believe Clara has been miscreant in her forcing Laura into a dalliance based upon blackmail. I feel sorry for Clara, but she has crossed a line which I can not condone."

Chablis smiled and said, "Lust makes us do some despicable things on occasion."

Smiling back at her, I said, "You should know!"

"Yeah, like you have never used that indelible Adam's charm to corral an innocent lass into your chamber. I know you Aaron Adams."

THE DISAPPEARANCE

I had no reply, just a shrug of the shoulders, for indeed, in my younger days, I was certainly guilty of many nefarious deeds to get a woman into my arms."

"Let us proceed as you have determined, and we shall accomplish something that it will be a life-long satisfaction to remember," she said. "However, you must be prepared for some twist of the screw which you do not anticipate. I never knew anything to go off just as one prognosticates it must."

With Chablis assurance of vigilance, I returned to my lodgings where I found the landlady waiting by the entrance. She asked how things were going and if the reward would be near at hand now. I smiled and assured her that all was on course and that she would have money in her hand soon. What is it about money that reaches the hearts of so many? If people could find the love for one another that they find for money what a wonderful world this could be. Alas, there appears to be no love like the love of money.

I uttered my goodbye to her and asked if any sound or disturbance had reached her ears from above. "Oh no, all is right up there; I've scarcely heard a whisper since you've been gone. In fact, it is unusually quiet for those two monstrous men."

THE DISAPPEARANCE

I gave her a knowing nod and meandered to my room. I left the door ajar and waited. Yes, I waited for the end of a most perplexing case.

CHAPTER 9

INVINCIBLE, IMPENETRABLE WALL

Next morning came a little note from Chablis. It had been left with the landlady who graciously handed it to me, saying that Chablis was the most alluring woman she had ever seen. I agreed and as she was leaving, I heard a noise next door and put the note down without reading it.

An hour passed; the doors of their rooms were closed as expected. A half hour more dragged its slow minutes away, and no sound had come from their precincts save now and then a mumbled word of parley between the father and son, a short command to the daughter, or a not-to-be-restrained oath of annoyance from one or both of the heavy-limbed brutes as something was said or done to disturb them in their indolent repose. At last my impatience was to be no longer restrained. Rising, I took a bold resolution. If the mountain would not come to Mohammad, Mohammad would go to the mountain. I deliberately proceeded to the door marked with the ominous red-cross and knocked.

A surprised snarl from within, followed by a sudden shuffling of feet as the two men leaped upright from what I presume had been a reclining position, warned me to be ready to face defiance if not the fury of despair as a result of their infamy.

"Ah miss," I said, as the door opened revealing in the gap her delicate face clouded with some new and sudden apprehension, "I beg your pardon but I am an older man, and I got a note today and my eyes are so weak with the work I've been doing that I cannot read it. It is from someone I love, and would you be so kind as to read off the words for me and so relieve an old man from his anxiety."

The murmur of suspicion behind her, warned her to throw wide open the door. "Certainly," said she, "if I can," taking the paper in her hand.

The paper was blank and she looked up at me bewildered. I gave her a smile and as her father came up, she quickly gave me the note.

THE DISAPPEARANCE

The father said, "What did it say."

She very demurely replied, "It said that he was to meet his daughter at the Park Avenue Hunter College Terminal today at 2 and to bring the $5000 with him." She winked at me and gently closed the door in my face. She knew they would follow me to steal the money and that would free her from them, so that she might make her way back to the Blake household.

I contacted Chablis and told her to be prepared to shadow me as I made my way uptown toward Hunter College. I said that we were about to entrap the two criminals, but that she should contact our friend John Havoc at the 87th Precinct and have him and whatever officers he deemed appropriate by her side. If he would be patient, he could not only apprehend them and return them to prison for their crime previously committed but catch them in the act of another crime, attempted murder, and see that they got at least another 25 years to life, which would assure two young people of a peaceful existence.

At exactly 2:00 PM, I walked out the door onto the landing and I heard the door behind me open and close. I descended the stairs and had a little grin as I walked out into the bright sunshine. I had them on the hook good.

THE DISAPPEARANCE

I spotted Chablis and John Havoc out of the corner of my eye as I walked under the arch on Washington Square. I wanted to make it simple for them to make their move, so I turned down an alley on the way to the subway station. They were pretty stupid. Without hesitation they stormed me, switchblades popped open, ready to stick me like a stuffed pig. Behind me, John shouted, gun in hand, "hands up."

Knives still in hand, they turned and stared at Chablis and John with drawn guns. John shouted, "Drop the knives or I will blow a hole so far up your ass you'll think you've been butt fucked by a gorilla."

They both glanced over their shoulders at me and I said, "Ever notice how you come across somebody once in a while you shouldn't have fucked with? That's me."

The father let out a scream, and throwing caution to the wind came at me. I shouted at Chablis and John to hold their fire as I set myself to meet the charge. Meanwhile, the son raised the blade and threw it at Chablis who squeezed off one round that ripped through his head and scattered brains all over the alleyway. The father was oblivious to what had occurred and only wanted the satisfaction of getting one blow in on me, even if it cost him his life. It did. I put out the heel of my right hand and that was it. I rammed his forehead so hard with the heel of my hand that his neck snapped and he collapsed. He lay there on the concrete, his head grotesquely twisted as his neck had snapped like a dead twig on a rotten tree.

I explained to John that we had pressing business at the Blake household, and he said we could drop by the precinct in a few hours and get things straightened out. We left the alley and headed for the Blake home.

Chablis looked over at me and said, "I am afraid that Laura will be a bit disappointed in the way things turned out. If she were an aristocrat, Laura would certainly represent the grandest tradition of noblesse oblige."

"Girl, don't throw your education at me. I know what that means – noble obligation. Let me bounce one off you Miss Intelligent. How about her tendency toward being a modern day Beau Geste?"

Chablis tilted her head in that alluring way, winked at me and said, "1939 movie with Gary Cooper. It means bold gesture or noble act. Gotcha!"

I laughed, shook my head and wondered how I got so lucky as to team up with the damn finest female detective in New York.

THE DISAPPEARANCE

When we got to the Blake house, to our surprise, standing across the street was Laura just staring at the house.

We walked over. Laura asked how her brother and father were. I did not have the courage to utter the words, but she knew. I reached in my pocket and took out a ring that I had found in the oven where the two had burned their prison clothes. "I traced this ring Laura. It is from a jewel robbery that occurred shortly after their escape. The owner of this ring was killed for it, but it was actually worthless, which they found out too late. Those two are murderers and you owe no loyalty to cold-blooded killers."

She sighed as Chablis placed her hand on her right shoulder and said, "Don't be afraid. Life is a gamble. You don't take a chance, nothing is going to happen. If necessary, you must risk everything for love."

Laura looked up at her and smiled. She said, "Will you two go with me."

We both nodded affirmatively and we all strolled across the street together to a house that had been for too long in the dark shadows of despair. Clara answered the door and tears filled her eyes, but words would not come. She was both delighted and ashamed.

THE DISAPPEARANCE

Laura reached out and said, "You loved me and lusted for me. That is not a crime. We shall forget all that has occurred and move forward as friends."

The tears were uncontrollable now. I moved forward and took Clara in my arms. "Your love for her brought her safely home. We need to see Mr. Blake."

Blake stood in the parlour completely speechless for what seemed many minutes, just staring at his bride. I said, "The miscreants are no more. All is rectified but the reconciliation of you two."

The two stood in silence. No doubt, looking at her, he could not understand why he had not recognized her before when she lived under his very roof.

Finally, Blake broke the silence. "I say it on the day of the discovery and the restoration of that wife for whom I have long searched, and to whom when found I have no word to give but sorry, sorry, sorry. You, Aaron and Chablis have restored my life."

With a deep smile, Laura bowed her head, "Let come what will, I can never again be unhappy knowing that you have been searching for me. Though you may send me away, I would go in the glorious knowledge that you searched for me, wanting to kindle that flame whose spark just needed lighting with your affection. That affection is all I desire in life. Tom, you are good; how good, I alone can know and duly appreciate who have lived in your house for so long now and I have seen with eyes that missed nothing, just what your surroundings are and have been from the earliest years of your proud life. But goodness must not lead you into the committal of an act you must and will repent to your dying day; or if it does, I who have learned my duty in the school of adversity, must show the courage and forbid what every secret instinct of my soul declares to be only provocative of shame and sorrow. You would take me to your heart as your wife; do you realize what that means?"

"I think I do," was his earnest reply. "Relief from heart-ache."

Her smooth brow wrinkled with a sudden spasm of pain but her firm lips did not quiver. "It means," she said, drawing nearer but not with that approach which indicates yielding, "it means, shame to the proudest family that lives in the land. It means knowledge of a past blotted by suggestions of crime; and apprehension concerning a future across which many tongues of deceit will wag. It means the hushing of certain words upon beloved lips; the turning of cherished eyes from visions of evil in my family. It means a home without the sanctity of memories; a husband without the honours he has been accustomed to enjoy; a wife with a fear gnawing like a serpent into her breast; and children, yes, perhaps children from whose innocent lips the sacred word of grandfather can never fall without wakening a blush on the cheeks of their parents."

"Tom," she continued, "I am weak to the voice of love pleading in my ear. But in one thing I am strong, and that is in my sense of what is due to the man I have sworn to honour. I left you because your pleasure and my own dignity demanded it; today I am back, but I come with many negatives by my side."

Tom pleaded. "My happiness is wrapped up in you, and I care not what comes. Let it come, and I shall face it with stiffened courage, because your love is all I desire."

"I might perhaps yield," she allowed with a faint smile. "But I love you as a girl brought up amid surroundings from which her whole being recoiled, but I must love the one who first brought light into my darkness and opened up to my longing mind to a life of culture, purity and honour. I come from stock that your family and friends would always have disdain for, and you know it."

THE DISAPPEARANCE

The prim and proper Mr. Blake shocked us all when he burst out with words one would never expect from him. "Fuck 'um all. I love you, and if they cannot understand that they have no place in my life. I may not have thought, certainly I did not realize, what I was doing when I rebuked you."

Still curious about the disappearance, Blake noticed a cut mark on Laura's wrist. "How did that occur?

"I found myself forced that night to inflict upon myself a little wound. They had heard you were a rich man, and the sight of the easy entrance to my chamber was too much for them to ignore. Indeed I know that it was for purposes of robbery they came, for they had hired this room opposite you some days previous to making the attempt. You see they were almost destitute of money and though they had some buried in the cellar of the old house in Vermont, they dared not leave the city to procure it. My brother was obliged to do so later, however. It was a surprise to them seeing me in your house. They had reached the roof of the extension and were just lifting up the corner of the shade I had dropped across the open window—I always open my window a few minutes before preparing to retire—when I rose from the chair in which I had been brooding, and turned up the heat. I was combing my hair at the time and so of course they recognized me. Instantly they gave a secret signal I, alas, remembered only too well, and crouching back, bade me put out the light that they might enter with safety. I was at first too much startled to realize the consequences of my action, and with some vague idea that they had discovered my retreat and come for purposes of advice or assistance, I did what they bid. Immediately they threw back the shade and came in, their huge figures looming frightfully in the faint light made by a distant street light. 'What do you want?' were my first words uttered in a voice I scarcely recognized for my own; 'why do you steal on me like this in the night? Aren't you afraid you will be discovered and sent back to the prison from which you have escaped?' Their reply sent a chill through my blood and awoke me to a realization of what I had done in thus allowing two escaped convicts to enter a house not my own. 'We want money and we're not afraid of anything now you are here.' And without heeding my exclamation of horror, they coolly told me that they would wait where they were until the household was asleep, when they would expect me to show them the way to the silver closet or what was better, the safe or wherever it was Mr. Blake kept his money. I saw they took me for a servant, as indeed I was, and for some minutes I managed to preserve that position in their eyes. But when in a sudden burst of rage at my refusal to help them, they pushed me aside and hurried to the door with the manifest intention of going below, I forgot prudence in my fears and uttered some wild appeal to them not to do injury to any one in the house for it was my husband's. Of course that disclosure had a profound effect."

"They stopped, but only to beset me with questions until the whole truth came out. I could not have committed a worse folly than thus taking them into my confidence. Instantly the advantages to be gained by using my secret connection with so wealthy a man for the purpose of blackmailing him seemed to strike both their minds at once, slow as they usually are to receive impressions. The silver-closet and money-safe sank to a comparatively insignificant position in their eyes, and to get me out of the house, and with my happiness at stake, treat with the honourable man who notwithstanding his non-approval of me as a woman, still regarded me as his lawfully wedded wife, became in their eyes a thing of such wonderful promise they were willing to run any and every risk to test its value. But here to their great astonishment I rebelled. Astonishment because they could not realize my desiring anything above money and the position to which they declared I was by law entitled. In vain I pleaded my love; in vain I threatened exposure of their plans if not whereabouts. The mine of gold which they fondly believed they had stumbled upon unawares, promised too richly to be easily abandoned. 'You must go with us,' they said, 'if not peaceably then by force,' and they actually advanced upon me, upsetting a chair and tearing down one of the curtains to which I clung. It was then I committed that little act cutting myself which you questioned me about. I wanted to show them I was not to be moved by threats of that character; that I did not even fear the shedding of my blood; and that they would only be wasting their time in trying to sway me by hints of personal violence. And they were a little impressed, sufficiently so at least to turn their threats in another direction, awakening fears at last which I could not conceal, much as I felt it would be policy to do so. Gathering up a few articles I most prized, my wedding ring, and a photograph of yourself that Ms. Luce had been kind enough to give me, I put on my bonnet and cloak and said I would go with them, since they persisted in requiring it. The fact is I no longer possessed motive or strength to resist. Even your unexpected appearance at the door, Clara, offered no prospect of hope. Arouse the house? What would that do? Only reveal my cherished secret and perhaps jeopardize the life of my husband. Besides, they were my own near kin, remember, and so had some little claim upon my consideration, at least to the point of my not personally betraying them unless they menaced immediate and actual harm. At the sight of a policeman in the street I made an effort to escape. But it was not successful. Though I was fortunate enough to free myself from the grasp of my father and brother, I reached the gate on the street only to encounter the eyes of him whose displeasure I most feared, looking sternly upon me from the other side. The shock was too much for me in my then weak and unnerved condition. Without considering anything but the fact that he never had known and never must, that I had been in the same house with him for so long, I rushed back to the corner and into the arms of the men who awaited me. How you came to be there, Tom, or why you did not open the gate and follow, I cannot say."

"The gate was locked," retorted Blake. "You remember it closes with a spring, and can only be opened by means of a key which I did not have."

"The next morning," Laura continued, "they put the case very plainly before me. I was at liberty to return at once to my home if I would promise to work in their interest by making certain demands upon you as your wife. All they wanted, said they, was a snug little sum and a lift out of the country. If I would secure them these, they would trouble me no more. But I could not concede to anything of that nature, of course, and the consequence was these long weeks of imprisonment and suspense; weeks that I do not now begrudge, seeing they have brought me the assurance of your esteem and the knowledge, that wherever I go, your thoughts will follow me with compassion if not with love."

We were all overwhelmed with the explanation, but it all put the pieces of an elaborate puzzle together. I looked at Blake and said, "I should have known the minute you told me and Chablis about the sojourn in the couple's cabin that this woman was your wife."

Chablis said, "What do you mean?"

I said, "What book Chablis was she reading when he saw her in the kitchen?"

"One by Hemingway."

"And of the many books we surveyed in her room. What was one of the author's names?"

Smiling knowingly and nodding her head, Chablis replied, "Hemingway."

Such a detailed story had not only exhausted Laura but those of us who listened so intently. We all let out a nearly simultaneous sigh of relief, but we were soon to find that there was much more to this story for we looked around and saw something that we had all overlooked.

First to notice it was Chablis who perused the room intently up, down, right and left. Then she took a deep breath and sighed.

I immediately caught on to what was on her furtive, detecting mind. It was then that Laura and Blake also must have caught on, for they, too, looked about the room and took in deep breaths.

I was the first one to utter the words: "Clara?"

Chablis simply said, "Clara?"

"Yes," said Blake, "where is Clara?"

And having told her story and thus answered his demands, Laura whispered, "Clara?" Then, she assumed once more the position of lofty reserve that seemed to shut Blake back from advance like she had erected an invincible, impenetrable wall.

CHAPTER 10

CLARA IS SOME WOMAN

Though we were all curious as to why Clara had left, Laura and Tom had to make sure they were on the same page about what lay ahead. Chablis said, "After all this, after all you have both suffered do you think either of you have a right to deny each other the desires of the heart?"

"My ideas of devotion," said Laura, "look beyond the present. It is to save him from years of wearing anxiety that I am leery to stick him with a wife such as I am."

He took a bold step forward. "Laura, you do not know a man's heart. To lose you now would not merely inflict a passing pain, but sow the seeds of a grief that would go with me to the grave."

"Do you then" she began, but paused blushing as Clara abruptly walked in.

"My dearest Annabelle. I mean Laura," said Clara, "you are wrong to hold out in this matter. I, who have honoured the family which I have so long served, above every other in the land, tell you that you can do it no greater good than to join it now, or inflict upon it any greater harm than to wilfully withdraw yourself from he who loves you."

Immediately Clara, whose emotion was genuine, plunged her hand into her pocket and drew out a folded paper. "Annabelle, Laura, I mean, if you could be convinced that you would be irretrievably injuring your husband and his interests, by persisting in that desertion of him which you purpose, would you not consent to reconsider?"

"If I could be made to see that, most certainly," returned she in a low voice whose broken accents betrayed at what cost she remained true to her resolve. "But I cannot."

"Perhaps the sight of this paper will help you, Clara said. And turning to Mr. Blake she exclaimed, "Your pardon for what I am called upon to do. A duty has been laid upon me which I cannot avoid, hard as it is for an old servant to perform. This paper, but it is more than just that you, sir, should see and read it first." And with a hand that quivered with fear or some equally strong emotion, she put it in his grasp.

The exclamation from Tom was bewildered. "Last will and testament by Harold Mortimer Blake."

"Executed under my eye," observed Clara.

His glance ran rapidly down the sheet and rested upon the final signature. "Why has this been kept from me?" he demanded, turning upon Clara with sternness.

"Your father asked it of me," was her reply. "His solemn and earnest command was that I keep the last will and testament which he gave into my care with his dying hands, a secret from the world. He said that at the expiration of that time mark if his son's wife sits at the head of her husband's table; if she does and is happy, suppress this by deliberately giving it to the flames, but if from any reason other than death, she is not seen there, carry it at once to my son, and bid him as he honours my memory, to see that my wishes as there expressed are at once carried out."

The paper in Mr. Blake's hand fluttered as he shook.

"You know what is written here?"

"I steadied his hand while he wrote," was her sad reply.

Mr. Blake turned with a look of inexpressible deference to his wife. "Madame," he said, "when I urged you with such warmth to join your fate to mine and honour my house by presiding over it, I thought I was inviting you to share the advantages of wealth as well as the love of a lonely man's heart. This paper destroys gratefully that illusion. Laura, the daughter-in-law of Harold Blake, is the one who by the inheritance of his millions has the right to command in this house. My father left his fortune to you."

With a cry she took from him the will whose purport was thus briefly made known. "Oh, how could he, how could he?" exclaimed Laura, running her eye down the sheet, and then crushing it spasmodically to her breast. "Did he not realize that he could do me no greater wrong?" Then in one yielding up of her whole womanhood to the mighty burst of passion that had been flooding the defences of her heart for so long, she exclaimed in a voice the mingled rapture and determination of which rings in my ears even now, "And is it a thing like this with its suggestions of mercenary interest that shall bridge the gulf that separates you and me? Shall the giving or the gaining of a fortune mean anything to me? No, no; by the smile with which your dying father took me to his breast, love alone, with the hope and confidence it gives, shall be the bond to draw us together and make of the two separate planes on which we stand, a common ground where we can meet and be happy. I love your father, but he was wrong to do this."

And with one supreme gesture, she tossed it into the burbling fire that crackled in the fireplace the will which she held, and sank all aglow into the joyous arms of he whom she loved.

I stood there watching the paper burn slowly and Clara smiled at me and walked out of the room.

As I prepared to leave a scene, perhaps the most gratifying in many respects that I had ever witnessed, I felt a slight touch on my arm. It came from Laura who with her husband had crossed the room to bid me farewell.

"Will you allow me to thank you," she said, "for the risk you two ran for me and of which I have just heard. It was an act that merits the gratitude of years, and as such shall be always remembered by me. If the old artist with the racking cough ever desires a favour at my hands, let him feel free to ask it. The interest I experienced in him in the days of my trouble, will suffer no abatement in these of my joy and prosperity." Then she looked at Chablis and said, "And to you also am I eternally grateful."

We spoke not but exited together, secure in the knowledge we had done a good deed for love. Chablis whispered to me as we walked out of the room, "You sly dog, you know something I don't."

Snickering just a bit, I said, "That will was written tonight. I saw the ink on it run as it was burning. Clara is some woman."

EPILOGUE

THAT'S ANOTHER TALE

Brent took a long, deep breath. The evening had been most enjoyable as the two old friends once again savoured with relish each others company. However, Aaron could tell there was something troubling him. He leaned forward, a soft drink in his hand and said, "O.K. Brent, old friend. What is it?"

"Well, the loose ends were all tied off very nicely, for the most part, and I must admit that your including some sex certainly made the story a bit more interesting. I must say that Chablis has always been a woman who has caught my interest, though, as an avowed Republican, I still am a bit in the wilderness when it comes to alternative lifestyles. Yet, I must admit to being a bit titillated with your vivid description of her sex with Cordell."

THE DISAPPEARANCE

Aaron eased back in his chair. "Yet, there is something else that is troubling you."

"Aaron there was one thing you left out, a detail which leaves a hole in the story, not a big one, but a small one at least - the cross by the door, what was its significance?"

Smiling, Aaron replied, "Ah, another night and another tale, my friend."

The End

Don't Miss These Aaron Adams Adventures

Fall from Apocalypse
Armageddon Now
Something Evil in the Darkness at Hopkins House
When Jesus Came to Jersey as the Son of Thunder
When Jesus Came to Canada
White Meteors and the Ghost of Sue Ann McGee
The Girl Who Stirred Up the Whirlwind
The Girl Who Motivated Murder Most Foul
The Girl Who Said Goodbye for the Last Time

And These Chablis Louise Chavez Mysteries

Chablis: Avenging Angel for the Forgotten
In the City of Lost Hope
Chablis and the Terrorist Who Resurrected
the Spirit of Che Guevara
Pursuit

www.ingramcontent.com/pod-product-compliance
Lightning Source LLC
Chambersburg PA
CBHW070816120626
46556CB00002B/536